For Searchers and Believers

and for Jessy Marie Gavlas; my gift of

sunshine.

ACKNOWLEDGEMENTS

T.L. Fernow for his diligent work, via long distance, in creating the cover for this book and providing much needed support through the difficult editing phase.

Joshua Karie for doing the photo shoot for the back cover. He showed great patience working with my fur beasts.

Alexia Carolann Johnson, for the artistic interpretation of the Fire Dragon in The Apache Story of Creation and for Owl Man in the story of Changing Woman. Lexi is a young, up and coming, and very talented artist who would like to have a career in the art field. I can see her illustrating for children's books right now!

Kim Wright Pritt for her years of friendship, being my "good luck charm" for over 50 years, and agreeing to write the "About the Author" section of this book. Kim is an excellent writer and maintains several different blogs such as the one for Albion Central School (our old Alma Mater), her church, and her personal blog where she shares her travels, movie reviews and life's inspirations @thoughtsbykim.com

The "real life" Jimmy Dale who shared his wisdom and love of life and was one of my muses for this story. He also created my turquoise inlaid walking sticks which help me treck the rugged Superstition terrain.

Ranger, Sniper, and Ruger, the mischievous pack that brings me laughter, love, peace and, in their own way, speak to me with great wisdom, love, and inspiration; if I am but willing to listen

THE SUPERSTITIONS AWAIT

We are, each of us born

Steeped in the flow of time.

To be outside of it all;

Then, why is that we wander,

rigged with such abstract minds?

Perhaps it is to imagine the traveling

possibilities of traveling

hard mountain veins and the anatomy

of unscarring one's own calloused fingertips

with nature's divine love;

She shows us how

an overzealous heart can bury

and resurrect us with the stomach-

dropping experience of simply

existing

"Don't give up"; She whispers

So let us find joy in this meager refusal,

because today: The Superstition Awaits

As we must wait

As the mountain has waited for us

there, on a cloudless day!

And through our eyes we actually "hear"

how far out and inside those jagged,

distant peaks must reach... in shadow

Somehow She has grasps the game of living

,

and plunges victory into our senses -

and all because of a single horizon's clarity

Her majesty

Her mystery.

Her magic.

The Superstition Mountains:

Able to see so far into suffering.

Into the vastness of so many eyes:

of ancient peoples and modern man.

It must expose so many of our iris-deep lies

to Her

Because She is not deceived,

and with slow haste She reaches across

distances

to solidify the strange emptiness

of the atoms beneath our feet

To direct us

Or to end us.

I grab my camera and with my beloved dog

start hiking, going off the designated way

We hurry down an isolated trail

the only sound, besides

our footsteps, is the moaning

of the wind through

the lonely canyons...

"The Voices of the Ancient Apache"

Superstitions' lore has said...

I want to capture that last glow

of light spread in its brilliant

splendor across the peaks

before its final flame

fades and sinks

into the night.

Surely, in a previous life

I was a Bedouin

The desert lives within my soul.

It's part of my sanguine flow.

Now I kneel in Superstition wilderness light

to touch the sacred soil.

Stone people keep watch over me,

A hawk is my trusted guide.

I want to spend eternity here

under the stars,

with Ranger by my side.

SEARCHING

*Even the ancient astronomers knew that the moon
blocks itself from us once every 29.5 days, moving into
position between the earth and the sun—the beginning
or the ending, a turn in the cycle watching the milky
way of stars move: footprints of the gods crossing the
roof of sky. The shield lifted,
we can touch the heavens.*

Hunter was gone now. The love of her life
had given up on life in the late summer of

1998. Since that time, she had looked
longingly and lovingly at the Superstition
Mountains from the park close to her
home; she could feel the pull of them on
her heart. Then, about 5 years later, with
the help of a good friend, she began to
travel out to them and to explore them.
For some unknown reason, this mountain
range called to her continuously. She
always felt that it carried some magical
force and, if she could just live within its
shadows, everything would be made right
again.

So, she began hiking frequently, whenever
time would permit in fact, and one of her
favorite places to hike was out past the
Peralta trail and Weaver's Needle. On her
third or fourth excursion into one of its

vast canyons (never remaining on established trails) she heard a delicate chime-like sound and decided that she wanted to hike down to the area from where it emanated. So, she began to make her way down the canyon.

Moving down into the heat of the canyon was oppressive. Most people fail to realize that the highest temperatures are found at the lowest elevations inside the canyon. Low relative humidity and generally clear skies mean that most of the sun's energy is available for daytime heating. These same conditions lead to rapid heat loss at night. However, she heard the gentle sound more clearly and decided it was worth the effort in order to search for the source of this delicate music.

With her pack on her back, she carefully let herself down into the steep canyon. Blue-black ravens dove above her while a fat horny lizard scurried at her feet. Watching the lizard, a bit too long, and forgetting where she was, she lost her footing and slid. Her hands braced the sharp dusty rocks to break her fall. Sliding to a stop, she caught her breath and quickly assessed the damage. Her hands were scuffed and bruises would probably come. Her manicure was ruined, but otherwise she was okay. In the back of her mind she could hear Jimmy Dale and Jon scolding her for hiking alone and in such dangerous areas...

"I know; I know"; she whispered; but I just can't help myself. It truly is the only way I feel at peace and whole"

She suddenly realized she was tired; exhausted in fact. "Enough adventures for one day", she said out loud to no one.

She drank from her "camel", letting the cool water knock some sense into her. Then she started back up the rugged canyon trail. The gentle, chime like music had stopped. But where had it come from?

"Maybe it was the reeds in a distant river?" she thought.

That sound would enter her world several times again and eventually the answer of where it came from would astound her.

Once she was out of the canyon, Elizabeth rested on a red boulder; the rock was cool against her hot skin. A small blue butterfly fluttered into the patch of silvery blue lupines nearby; these lupines had already begun to produce hairy seed pods. The butterfly flitted nervously around the remaining indigo flowers. Liz noticed the white arrowhead markings under its tattered violet-blue wing: a male arrowhead blue -- a very rare species, especially here at the edge of this desert

range. This one was patrolling the
flowers for just one more chance to mate;
while a handful of caterpillars from
earlier mating's were already munching
on flowers and fruits.

"Time.

It runs

Then hesitates...

Cries catch me

But won't wait.

Elizabeth softly whispered to it: "Last
year's crop is in the past now, you gentle
thing; best you go home before the
weather changes"

Finding no mates here, and not heeding her sage advice, the butterfly flew off in search of lupines and mates elsewhere...

Smiling sadly to herself, Elizabeth wished it good luck as she knew how hard it was to be alone; one is constantly searching for that which is lost or which has been stolen.

Turning around slowly, she headed back up the trail...

PREMONITIONS

"Since the time of St. Jerome, it was mandatory for any
kind of
Scholar or thinker to spend time out in the desert in
solitude.
It's no coincidence that the desert has been a major
part of the
Visionary or mystical experience from the beginning of
time"
~Bill Viola~

It was something about the immense longing in Elizabeth's soul --something to do with the constant "waking dreams" and the time for deep thoughts that brought them on -- that led her to places of solitude like the Superstitions. This was probably why the desert life suited her so well. The quiet time, without nagging cell phones and the interminable media flow we're subjected to in these modern -- these so-called "better" times.

It was during such times that the "dreams" would come. Ever since she was a very little girl, dreams and premonitions would come -- filled with people she had known or thought she knew, and places she was sure she'd seen.

Sometimes they would be places that she wouldn't know until much later in life; but they always were so familiar.

When she was very little she would spend a great deal of time alone out in her play house; a full two room attachment to her father's garage which he had set aside for her and her older sister to use as their childhood retreat. Or you could find her in the shade of a cherry tree in whose branches she sought solace in the spring, summer and early fall. At times during these solitary moments, she would dream; not the dreams of restful sleep, but vivid and detailed living dreams. Quite often she had dreamed of the death of a family member days before it actually occurred. This frightened her mother and her godmother when they realized that every time she told them that someone was going to die soon; they did. Elizabeth soon learned to keep those dreams to herself.

Once, she had dreamed of an airplane circling for hours above a busy airport unable to put its wheels down and woke up feeling the intense, gut wrenching fear of the passengers. Then while she was traveling home alone from England as a young teen, her plane was forced to belly land in Heathrow airport when the landing gear failed to come down despite every attempt by the pilots and the ground crew. The fear of the passengers permeated the cabin of that plane just as it had done in her dream several months prior. For some reason, Liz had not felt any panic at all. She already knew the outcome.

She had dreamed of the little white house she and Hunter had settled in when they were expecting their first child in Virginia; months before they ever saw the property and in such extreme detail. And she had dreamed of the birth of their first child that would be born in that house; that it would be a son. How she had loved that clapboard house with its huge kitchen, its large spacious two bedrooms and the potbellied stove in the living room that would heat the house so toasty warm in the cooler Virginia months. The yard was over ½ acre and she had a clothes line which was great for hanging out diapers to dry in the sun and wind. Two basset hounds, Happy and Rocky (named after the Rockefellers) ran freely and sometimes noisily through the yard and house, And of course, their first born had been a son... a beautiful "golden child"

She remembered seeing the vivid, painful flash of her life alone without Hunter, when the Groom Wedding Goblet from the set they had received on their wedding day, fell from Hunter's hand and shattered into glittering shards as they celebrated their 23rd Wedding Anniversary. This had occurred a little over a year before his death. He had laughed when he saw the worried

expression in her eyes and called it
superstitious mumbo jumbo…

"I am not going to die any time soon", he
had told her, hugging her tightly as the
tears welled up into her eyes. "That
superstitious nonsense your family fed
you about toasting goblets is just that,
NONSENSE! Just because a glass breaks
does NOT mean I am going to die. "

"But I'm not superstitious, Hunter"; she
had said. "I do, however, believe in
prophecy and signs."

The dream she had on that night terrified
her! How she wished that one sign in
particular had not come true. She had
tried so very hard to make it NOT come

true. She tried everything she knew to want him to be healthier and to give up the negative components of his life. She had failed and that failure haunted her still.

Then one day, while she was traveling with her oldest and youngest children to a friend's home for an open house, she had a vision of being abandoned by her children and left alone in a ghetto. Sadly, this too came true as the condominium property where she had rented a home, fell into neglect and disrepair and the children, due to ignorance and lack of communication, left her alone and ill.

She saw her mother, alone in a colorless, loveless hospital room, crying; calling for her daughter and asking why? She felt the pain of not being able to take her hand, console and comfort her or explain. The next day a friend texted her off of Facebook and asked her for her phone number. Liz had told Alice that there was no need to make the phone call... she already knew. Her mother had died... alone, in a hospital room. Her mother had always been afraid of being put in "home". The guilt Liz felt over this could not be assuaged.

Although she rarely remembered her dreams (as we all dream nightly and generally several times in a night), when she did, it was the ones which were of a vivid movie-length, and she would remember each piece of it. The dreams often had a soundtrack, and each grain of sand, or rock, or plant was intricate in their details.

One of the things Elizabeth learned when she began hiking in Arizona was that hours spent in silence in the desert created the weighty hush of a cathedral. The longer you sat making no noise, the harder it was to break the quiet. If you didn't want to be found you didn't make noise. If you were tired of the closeness of the people around you, you walked out into the saguaro forest and then you didn't make a sound. This was her place to escape the stress and pain of daily life.

Once, while hiking through the Superstitions on a late fall day, she paused to rest and actually fell asleep behind a creosote bush in a place she liked to visit to get away from the chaos of the far too busy world. She wedged herself between two bushes and the branches swayed over her, creating a perfect hiding spot and sat down to rest and meditate. The sand was finely ground and soft as a pillow; a rare find in the hard desert ground. Gradually she fell asleep and sometime later was awakened by a sound.

Initially Elizabeth had kept her eyes shut tightly; sensing as if even the movement of opening them would draw attention. She heard soft padding in the sand, and then the sound of panting like a dog; a rather large dog. She froze. It must be a coyote! Although Elizabeth wasn't afraid of them, she knew they were unpredictable and what if it had rabies? Also, the coyote is known as the Trickster in Indian Lore and is not to be trusted. The sound paused, as if the creature had sensed something.

She opened her eyes as quietly as she could. Nothing...

Removing the knife from her belt she soundlessly slithered out from her hiding place.

Nothing... The smooth sand held no trace of any prints other than her own. The desert was silent.

A dog ghost, then?" she whispered. "A
spirit of the Mountain?"

One of these "dreams" was a reoccurring
one which she had started having several
years ago; before she started living such a
grounded "default" life, as city dwellers
term it. You know, the life full of "reality",
and 9 to 5 structured hours, and boring
people; that stock happiness with
everything she supposedly needed but
with so very little that she actually
wanted. She would admonish herself
NOT to feel ungrateful and tell herself;
"this is what everyone wants". *(Sadly, she
could never quite convince that little desert
rat gypsy soul who lived inside her that any
of this was what **she wanted**.)*

In this reoccurring "dream", she was walking in the desert as the sun went down. The light reflected from cliffs with a warm golden glow, the purple shadows lengthening toward her as if trying to embrace her; or ensnare her. She stooped and picked up a few rocks, rolling them in the palm of her hand as she often did when hiking. She felt their roughness and watched the dust drift down from them.

People say when you're dreaming to look for details, to pick up a leaf and try to see its veins, to look at your hand and see if the lines are there. Dreams supposedly can't hold this level of detail, and you will know you are dreaming. Every detail she looked for was there; as it was with every

dream that turned into a premonition --
that turned into reality.

She kept walking and, just over a rise,
spotted the ruins of a dwelling among the
boulders. It was the same color as the
desert around it, and hard to see. When
she walked down the hill and found the
low-entry opening on the other side, she
bent and went inside. On a pallet, looking
up at the hole in the roof, was an old
Native Indian man; an eagle feather in his
hair. He wore a buckskin shirt, faded torn
blue jeans, work boots and a mysterious,
impish smile.

"Look," he said. "A Sipapu! They're
everywhere and they are nowhere."

Then, he reached out his hand and stuck it through the solid rock wall of the ruin. His arm disappeared up to the elbow. He looked over and motioned her to follow and then he, too, was gone.

Without a moment's hesitation, Elizabeth tried to follow him, and stuck her head straight through the wall. For a few brief moments, she glimpsed a world of shadowy light and an empty plain far out into the distance.

At exactly that point, EVERY single time, she would awaken; shaking in wonder and excitement! She would also be very cold despite the warmth of her bedroom and it would take her some time to warm up.

After that first initial dream, she looked up the word the old Indian had said; Sipapu. "Sipapu" is a Native American word for a small hole the Indian people would build in the floor of their wikiups, to symbolize the portal their ancestors entered this world through, from the destroyed underworld. It is also used to describe vortexes or entry points into other dimensions; some believe between here and the spirit world.

"I know that vortexes -- Sipapu exist, I know they do" Elizabeth said to herself. "One day, I will find one."

PORTALS AND SIPAPU

"There is no death

Only a change of worlds..."

~Chief Seattle~

Long before prospectors came to town

digging for gold, indigenous tribes knew

the Superstitions as the sacred setting of

their creation myths and as a source for evil.

In the Hopi story of the Emergence, the first humans came up from an underground city through hidden portals deep within the mountains called Sipapu. From here they entered the Fourth World, the world in which we all live today.

The Pima also have a story about a man and his wife who withstood a great flood by building an ark which deposited them right on top of Superstition Mountain. They also believe that an evil spirit lurks behind its peaks.

The Apache dubbed this mountain range the Devil's Playground and believed their

Thunder God lived inside. Anyone who disrespected their god by trespassing on his land, or who attempted to take something away with the mountains, was surely doomed.

Ask around today, and local residents will tell you stories about strange lights hovering in the sky above the mountains that disappear in the blink of an eye. This was apparently true as on four separate occasions her friend, Jon, had actually seen a couple of them during his visits out to Arizona and photographed them. In his photos, they were cylindrical shapes that followed no exact pattern; seeming to hover and then zip away.

The locals also talk about energy "vortexes" that take your breath away and pull on your body; making it feel like it's made out of lead or like it is trying to turn itself inside out. Elizabeth had felt these herself and wondered if that was meant by the term "sucking the life" out of someone because that is actually what it felt like to her.

Just like the tales that her friend Jimmy Dale had told her over the years, the locals also said that there are portals out in Superstitions that can move from one place to another and make it possible for people to experience time and dimensional shifts. Near the winter and spring solstices, people have also seen swirling dense black shapes that pass right through them; leaving them chilled to the bone.

Many will continue to tell you about a series of secret underground tunnels running beneath the mountains. Still others will point to the old military trail that supposedly runs right by the Lost Dutchman's mine and talk about a government conspiracy of the highest order and the possibility of ancient aliens being secluded below.

The one thing Elizabeth had learned for certain over the past 18 years was that if you spend enough time out there -- even the most skeptical human being will come to believe that there is something going on in those mountains; something beyond scientific explanation.

Jimmy Dale, as well as most other Native American's in the area and "believer" historians, were certain of the existence of the Sipapu. So was Elizabeth.

History and Warnings

"The past speaks to us in a thousand voices,
warning and comforting, animating and stirring
to action." ~Felix Adler~

The Superstition mountains rise three thousand feet above the landscape, and have a dramatic beauty about them - an ever changing beauty that Elizabeth just can't take her eyes away from when she is driving east on the 60 or the 202. To be truthful, whenever she was within view of these mountains, even from a park or her own back door, she was mesmerized by them.

The fact is, their history alone is well worth exploring. As far as anyone can determine, the first inhabitants of the Superstition Mountain area may have arrived here as much as 5000 years ago. The Hohokam and Mogollon Indian cultures flourished in the area more than two thousand years ago, and the Salado

Indians inhabited the area from 1000 A.D. to 1400 A.D.

The Superstitions are a place where time has refused to adhere to man-made rules, and seems to do its own thing in absolute defiance of man. If you keep an open mind, this is a place where you will experience one phenomenon after the next, and it can be devastating to the weak of heart or mind. It is important to know yourself well and to keep a deep respect for the desert - or she will swallow you alive. If you do not believe in supernatural experiences before you wander here, you will after you leave. The Apache named this mountain terrain "the Devils playground" and for good reason.

Elizabeth's dear friend, ever since arriving here in AZ almost 20 years ago, was a half breed Apache named Jimmy Dale. Nearing 80 and silver haired, his eyes still sparkled in a sun dried face. An accomplished hunter, hiker, craftsman and story teller, he taught her so much about the desert flora and fauna, the rapid changes of temperature and terrain, and a great respect for the magical, spiritual qualities of the Superstitions.

"It is said," he told her, "that Geronimo would be seen walking into the face of the Mountain, disappearing and then reappearing in New Mexico. The soldiers, who were hell bent on capturing the illusive Apache Chief, were mystified as to how he was able to escape the human net surrounding him and his band."

 Jimmy continued; "The Apache have a legend that their remote ancestors came from a large island in the eastern sea where there were great buildings and ports for ships. However, the Fire Dragon arose, and their ancestors had to flee their beautiful city to mountains far away to the south. In order to survive, they were finally forced to take refuge in immense and ancient tunnels through which they

wandered for years." And then he told her this tale of the Apache Creation Story:

"Geronimo's Story of the Creation of the Apache":

"In the beginning the world was covered with darkness. There was no sun, no day. The perpetual night had no moon or stars.

There were, however, all manner of beasts and birds. Among the beasts were many hideous, nameless monsters, as well as dragons, lions, tigers, wolves, coyote, beavers, rabbits, squirrels, rats, and all manner of creeping things such as lizards and snakes. Mankind could not gain a foot-hold under such conditions, for the beasts and snakes destroyed all human offspring.

All creatures had the power of speech and were gifted with intelligence.

There were two tribes of creatures: the birds or the feathered tribe and the beasts. The birds were organized with their chief, the eagle.

These tribes often held councils, and the birds wanted light admitted. This the beasts repeatedly refused to allow. Finally, the birds made war against the beasts.

The beasts were armed with clubs, but the eagle had taught his tribe to use the bow and arrow. However, the serpents were so wise that they could not all be killed. One took refuge in a perpendicular cliff of a mountain in Arizona, and his eyes (changed into a brilliant stone) and may be seen in that rock to this day.

The bears, when killed, would each be changed into several other bears, so that the more bears the feathered tribe killed, the more there were

The dragon could not be killed, either, for he was covered with four coats of horny scales, and the arrows would not penetrate these.

One of the most hideous, vile monsters (that was nameless) was also protected against arrows, so the eagle flew high up in the air with a round, white stone, and let it fall on this monster's head, killing him instantly. This was such a good service that the stone was called sacred. They fought for many days, but at last the birds won the victory.

After this war was over, although some evil beasts remained, the birds were able to control the councils, and light was admitted; then mankind could survive and prosper. The eagle was chief in this good fight: therefore, his feathers are now worn by man as emblems of wisdom, justice, and power.

Among the few human beings that were then alive was a woman who had been blessed with many children, but these had always been destroyed by the beasts. If by any means she succeeded in eluding the other evil creatures, the dragon, who was very wise and extremely evil, would come himself and eat her babies.

After many years, a son of the Rainstorm was born to her and she dug for him a deep cave. The entrance to this cave she closed and over the spot built a camp fire. This concealed the child's hiding place and kept him warm. Every day she would remove the fire and descend into the cave where the child's bed was to nurse him; then she would return and rebuild the campfire.

Frequently the dragon would come and question her, but she would say,

"I have no more children; you have eaten all of them."

When the child was larger he would not always stay in the cave, for he sometimes wanted to run and play. Once, the dragon saw his tracks, which perplexed and enraged the old dragon since he could not find the hiding place of the boy; but he said that he would destroy the mother if she did not reveal the child's hiding place. The poor mother was very much troubled; she could not give up her child, but she knew the power and cunning of the dragon and therefore she lived in constant fear.

Soon after this the boy said that he wished to go hunting. The mother would not give her consent. She told him of the dragon, the wolves, and snakes; but he said, "Tomorrow I go!"

At the boy's request, his uncle (who was the only man living at that time) made a little bow and some arrows for him, and the two went hunting the next day. They trailed the deer far up the mountain and finally the boy killed a buck. His uncle showed him how to dress the deer and prepare the meat. They broiled two hind quarters, one for the child and one for his uncle. When the meat was done they placed it on some bushes to cool. Just then the huge form of the dragon appeared. The child was not afraid, but his uncle was so frozen with fear that he did not speak or move.

The dragon took the boy's parcel of meat and walked away with it. He placed the meat on another bush and seated

himself beside it.

Then he said, "So you are the child I have been seeking. Boy, you are nice and fat, so when I have eaten this venison I shall eat you."

The boy said, "No, you shall not eat me, and you shall not eat that meat." So he boldly marched over to where the dragon sat and took the meat back to his own resting place.

The dragon said, "I like your courage, but you are foolish; what do you think you could do against the likes of me? "

"Well," said the boy, I can do enough to protect myself, as you may soon find out."

Then the dragon took the meat again, and then the boy immediately took it back. Four times the dragon took the meat, and after the fourth time that the boy took back the meat he said, "Dragon, will you fight me?"

The dragon said, "Yes, in whatever way you like."

The boy said, "I will stand one hundred paces distance from you and you may have four shots at me with your bow and arrows; provided

*that you will then exchange places
with me and give me four shots."*

*"Done", growled the dragon. "Take
your position; arrogant one."*

*Then the dragon took his bow, which
was made of a large pine tree. He
took four arrows from his quiver;
they were made of young pine tree
saplings, and each arrow was twenty
feet in length. He took deliberate
aim, but just as the arrow left the
bow the boy made a peculiar sound
and leaped into the air. Immediately
the arrow was shattered into a
thousand splinters, and the boy was
seen standing on the top of a bright
rainbow over the spot where the*

dragon's aim had been directed.
Soon the rainbow was gone and the
boy was standing on the ground
again.

Four times this was repeated, and
then it was the boy's turn.
"Dragon, stand here in my place; it is
my turn to shoot!"

The dragon sneered, "All right, but
your little arrows cannot pierce my
fine coats of horn. Go ahead --shoot
away."

The boy shot an arrow, striking the
dragon just over the heart, and one
coat of the great horny scales fell to
the ground. With the next shot

another coat dropped off, and then another, and finally the dragon's heart was exposed. Then the dragon trembled in fear, but could not move.

However, before the fourth arrow was shot the boy noticed his uncle frozen to the exact same spot he had been in when the dragon first approached.

He called out, "Uncle, you are frightened almost to death! You have not moved since this battle began. Come here beside me or the dragon will fall on you and you will die!"

His uncle ran toward him. Then the boy shot the fourth arrow with true aim, and it pierced the dragon's heart. With a tremendous roar the dragon rolled down the mountain side, down four precipices, into a canyon below.

Immediately storm clouds swept the mountains, lightning flashed, thunder rolled, and the rain poured down in torrents. When the rainstorm finally passed, far down in the canyon below, they could see fragments of the huge body of the dragon lying among the rocks. The bones of this dragon may still be found there today.

*The boy's name was **Apache**.*

Having brought his Chosen One through this fearsome trial, Usen, the Great Creator, then taught him how to prepare herbs for medicine, how to hunt, and how to fight. He was the first chief of the Indians and wore the eagle's feathers; the sign of justice, wisdom, and power. To him and to his people, as they were created, Usen gave homes in the land of the West."

Elizabeth loved this particular story and wondered if this is where Geronimo's knowledge came from regarding the talked of tunnel system of the Superstitions? Were his people actually forced to live beneath the earth for eons? Did they, one day, just walk through a portal and populate the earth? Were some of them still down there? She had so many questions running through her mind.

She also learned of other legends about the rumored tunnel systems of the Superstitions. Some said they were dangerous and inhabited by Reptilian-like Creatures or aliens, and other supernatural forces.

Those that claim to have actually entered the tunnel system tell of the remains of ancient structures and a spiral staircase that leads forever down into the bowels of earth.

"Perhaps", Elizabeth thought, "the mouth of hell?"

Per some of the stories and legends, the main entrance to the Superstition tunnel system links to numerous tunnel passageways which spider web out as far as Central America and one can travel beneath the earth's surface for thousands of miles. Oh, how Elizabeth longed to find at least one of these passage ways. Would one of them, just one of them, pierce that thin veil between this life and the next? She had yet to find a single real tunnel.

TERROR AND DEATH

"We have the right hand that strikes and makes for evil, and we have the left hand full of kindness, near the heart, one foot may lead us to an evil way, the other foot may lead us to a good... "~ Eagle Chief Letakos-Lesa ~

Jimmy Dale also taught her much more of the history of the Apache and the Yavapai; history lessons that let her understand the reason the Superstitions held not only mystery and magic but in some instances—**terror and death.**

According to the history that Jimmy Dale knew, the Rancheria Campaign occurred in the Superstition Mountain area. Between 1864 and 1868, the Rancheria Campaign against the Apache and Yavapai eventually ended much of the hostilities along the Gila and Salt Rivers. Prior to the cattlemen's use of this valley, which continues to some degree today, it was an important Native American encampment or farmstead. During the 1860s the Apache and Yavapai had a Rancheria in the valley. This village was used on an intermittent basis because of the water supply. When water was abundant the

Native Americans grew maize, beans and squash along Tortilla Creek.

The Apaches and Yavapai had a nasty habit of raiding their distant neighbors along the Salt and Gila River for women and supplies. Prior to 1860 there was very little the Pima Indians could do to prevent these raids. It was certain death to challenge the Apache in their mountain sanctuary to the east, and the Pima avoided these mountains because the region was the home of their dreaded enemy.

This all changed when John D. Walker settled along the banks of the Gila River near what is now Florence in early 1860. Walker soon organized a loose-knit

militia of Pima Indians and white settlers
to combat the problematic raids of the
Apache and Yavapai and the "1st Arizona
Volunteers" was formed. The Territorial
Governor John N. Goodwin commissioned
Walker a lieutenant and promised to help
with supplies.

Walker's first campaign against the
Apache-Yavapai consisted of several
attacks by his poorly armed group of
volunteers. Even under such conditions
this rag-tag militia struck hard against the
Apache-Yavapai Rancherias in the Pinal
Mountains. The first campaign consisted
of approximately 200 Pima scouts and
forty American settlers. Camp McDowell
was established along the Verde River in
1864 to control the predatory raids of the

Apache-Yavapai from Tonto Basin down to the Salt River and into the Salt River Valley. Units from under the command of Colonel Bennett went into the field in 1866 and continued operations until the end in 1868. Their mission was to eliminate hostile villages in the Tonto Basin area, the Pinal Mountains and the Superstition Mountains.

On May 11, 1866, Lt. John D. Walker led members of the 14th and 24th infantries against both the Apache and the Yavapai in what is now known as the Superstition Wilderness. Their mission was to destroy all Native American villages or Rancherias and capture or kill all inhabitants they could find south of the Salt River, north of the Gila River and east of the Superstition

Mountains. Walker turned southward from the Salt River at a place called Mormon Flat and then followed Tortilla Creek into the mountains.

Jimmy Dale sadly told Elizabeth; "His column first attacked a large encampment of Native Americans above Hell's Hole on Tortilla Creek. The infantry unit killed 15 warriors at Hell's Hole and then moved up Tortilla Creek to Dismal Valley. Walker's command attacked a large Rancheria in Dismal Valley killing 57 Indians, including several women and children.

During the clean-up operation, the mosquitoes were so fierce, the stench of the dead so nauseating, and the heat so extreme that the site became known as "Dismal Valley".

Walker led several other campaigns into the Superstition Mountain area during the period from 1860 to 1868. Although the Apaches no longer live in the Apache Junction/Goldfield/Superstition area (they moved further north to the White Tanks Mountains), you can, if you sit up near the top of the Superstition, and remain very still, almost hear their chants; their cries and the sounds of battle and mourning."

Elizabeth knew the truth of that statement. Often, during her hikes up to Flat Iron, she would sit alone and hear those sounds moaning through the canyons

"Later, in 1875, the United States military forced the removal of an estimated 1500 Yavapai and Tonto Apache from the Rio Verde Indian Reserve and its several thousand acres of treaty lands promised to them by the United States government. Under the orders of the Indian Commissioner, L.E. Dudley, Army troops made the people, young and old, walk through winter-flooded rivers, mountain passes and narrow canyon trails to get to the Indian Agency at San Carlos, which was over 180 miles away. The hard journey resulted in the loss of several hundred lives; this was the Apache' Trail of Tears."

"The people were forced to remain there, against their will, for 25 years while white settlers took over their land; only a few hundred ever returned.

"According to one Apache legend", Jimmy Dale told her, "the portal leading down into the lower world is located right here in the Superstitions. Winds blowing from the hole supposedly cause the great dust storms that plague the Valley particularly during the monsoon season. Some Apaches who converted to Christianity believed that the portal was the entrance to hell and that the Superstitions were the place where the devil dwelled.

He added; "It is why we still believe today that there are many portals (or vortexes) here, and spirit faces to be found in the rocks. Some are just that, spirit faces, but some -- are not."

"Now, I am not making any claims as to what or who might have created them, but I assure you that these portals do exist, and it is not exactly like taking a walk through the park to enter one of these. If you do come across one, keep in mind that if you can pass through, then something else can pass through going in the opposite direction. Keep in mind also that some vortexes are stationary while others are moving.

Elizabeth looked at him in disbelief.

"Yes, you heard correctly, I said moving -- as in from one location to another; like waves of energy. Also they are not always accessible, some are open all the time; most, however, are not. So... if you went through one, there is no guarantee it will be open when or even if you return."

Several times, during their long hikes together along the Peralta Trail or heading towards Weavers Needle or Tortilla Flats, Elizabeth would feel as if something was softly touching her or she would see something appear, just out of the corner of her eye, only to have it disappear if she abruptly turned around to see it close up. Then, too, there was always that gentle chime-like murmur that apparently only she could hear...

Jimmy Dale advised her; "Nothing should come to any great surprise to you in the

Superstitions Mountain wilderness. Don't be shocked if in one minute you turn about to see an old Indian or prospector standing in the distance starring at you...or even a little person. You blink your eyes and 'they've disappeared'. That's part of the norm. Or you find that you are missing time you cannot account for and then reach into your pocket to find a piece of gold or crystals that you KNOW **you** did not pick up. That, my friend, is also normal of the Superstitions and its Sipapu."

"The Superstition Mountains are also notorious for the many bizarre deaths and be-headings that have taken place there. Many have said that in certain parts of this desert wilderness a sudden force or irrational impulse can come over a person and cause them to suddenly turn against others in their party. There have been several cases where strange 'voices' have driven treasure-hunters insane and, in some instances, driven them to kill their partners and even their own families."

"Then too, there are strange reports of the ghost like figure dubbed the "Borego Phantom" roaming the mountain range. It is said to appear to gold-seekers and then only after darkness falls. Some who have seen it said the phantom manifests itself as an 8-foot tall human skeleton with a lantern in its chest. Many believe it is the ghost of a prospector."

"One thing is for certain", Jimmy Dale gravely added, "far too many lives have been taken by these mountains. Don't you become one of its victims! Respect the Thunder god and the curse of the Apache -- for they are real; as real as you and me!"

The one thing that he always cautioned her about, over and over again (other than understanding that everything in the desert either poked, stung, or bit and to carry a great deal more water than you think you will need), was to NEVER REMAIN THERE AFTER DARK!

"Things happen here that cannot be explained"; he cautioned. "Here the veil that separates this world from others must be extremely thin, for the access to inner Earth and the spiritual realm is almost an open field. In the space of a day a person can experience several different time and dimensional shifts, with temperatures reaching over 130 degrees in the day and dropping to 32 degrees, or below, in a matter of a few hours as the sun sets."

Since Elizabeth so loved her sunsets and the immense star filled skies the Superstitions offered, she always failed to listen to that warning. So far, nothing bad had happened and she had seen so many glorious things. So far.

"It is too beautiful not to stay to see"; she whispered to herself.

CURSE OF THE THUNDERGOD

"Terrified by the "Thunder God" illuminating wrath
on who's sacred ground we trespassed, while
names, utterances of our mouths, clinging to our lips, as
language wriggles in and out, while mythological tongues
put fire on our foreheads."

Many skeletons have been found in the
Superstitions; sometimes missing their
heads. The horrifying history of those

who went in search of the gold or tried to take anything on the Thunder god's mountain should give any sensible person pause in deciding if they want to travel this mystical but deadly area. Jimmy Dale warned Elizabeth numerous times NEVER to take ANYTHING off of the mountain as it angered the spirits that ruled there.

"When you travel through the Thunder god's realm, take nothing, not so much as a rock or a flower and leave behind only your footprints. Do no desecrate the ground in any fashion"; Jimmy Dale warned her.

The legends of the lost mine, but more importantly the tales of the Apache curse which were meant to protect anything on (or in) the Mountains, have continued to grow over the years and mysterious deaths and disappearances are often attributed to these stories:

For instance, in the summer of 1880, two recently discharged soldiers from Fort McDowell, came to the mountains looking for work in the Silver King Mine where they showed a bag of gold ore to the manager, Aaron Mason. Stunned at the quality of the ore, he immediately asked the soldiers where they found it and they told him by an old mine in the Superstitions. So, Mason entered into a partnership with them and provided them with the necessary provisions to mine the area productively. They headed out towards Weaver's Needle but a little

more than two weeks later, their nude
bodies were found; both shot in the head.

Then, there is the story about Elisha
Marcus Reavis, known as the: "Madman of
the Superstitions" or "Old Hermit", who
was actually a highly educated college
student who had taught school before he
began to prospect. (Considering the fact
that he did not mind meeting with
journalists and apparently "hired help",
Liz wondered how he could have been
deemed a true hermit at all.)

However, it was not his manner that
earned him these titles; it was his
appearance, his high intelligence and the
isolated say he chose to live. He never cut
his hair or shaved, seldom bathed, and it

was rumored he was prone to running naked through the canyons firing his pistol into the sky. Even the Apache left him alone as they felt that madmen were somehow in the presence of God.

Then, in the spring of 1896, after he had not been seen for some time, one of his few friends went looking for him. The 70-year-old Reavis was found dead four miles south of his home; his severed head lying several feet away from his naked body.

Later that same year, two men from the eastern part of the country went in search of the mine; they were never heard from again.

In 1910, the skeleton of a woman was found in a cave high up on Superstition Mountain. With the body were several pieces of gold. The cause of her death was never determined.

In 1927, a New Jersey man and his sons were hiking the mountain when rocks began to roll down on them from the bluffs above. It was as if someone were pushing the boulders the man had told family and friends. One of the boy's legs was crushed.

A year later, two deer hunters were literally driven off the mountain when boulders, which again appeared to have been pushed by someone or "something", came rolling down the mountain towards them.

In the summer of 1931, Adolph Ruth, a Washington DC veterinarian and avid treasure hunting hobbyist went missing in the wilderness area of the peak. Six months later, in December, a skull with two holes in it was discovered by an archeological expedition near the three Red Hills; the skull was that of Adolph Ruth. The rest of his body was not found until January in a small tributary on the east slope of Black Top Mesa.

Although the headlines were sensational and alluded to the probability that Ruth had been murdered for his treasure map, the coroner was not positive that the holes in the skull were from bullets. However, his son Erwin, was absolutely convinced that foul play had been involved.

Most believe that Ruth died from the extreme desert heat and that his body had been carried away in parts by wild animals. Still others felt that the mountain's curse had claimed another life.

The Superstitions claimed the life of Adam Stewart in 1934, cause of death listed as unknown.

Two years later, in 1936, another life was claimed by the Mountain. Hobbyist Roman O 'Hal, a New York Broker, died

from a fall when he went searching for
the lost mine.

James Cravey, a prospector, made a highly
publicized trip into the Superstition
Canyon's in the summer of 1947 via
helicopter. The pilot set him down in La
Barge Canyon, which is very close to
Weaver's Needle. However, when he
failed to hike out as planned a search
party sent looking for him and although
they found his camp, he was not there.
The following February his headless
skeleton was found in the canyon. It was
tied in a blanket and his skull was found
about thirty feet away. Strangely the
coroner's jury ruled that there was "no
evidence of foul play."

In early 1953, Joseph Kelley from Dayton, Ohio went in search of the lost mine. He vanished, never to be seen alive again. Two years later, his body was discovered near Weaver's Needle. The shot in his skull was ruled an accidental shooting incident.

That same year, two California boys, went out on a hike in the Superstition Mountains and vanished. Unfortunately, NOTHING was ever found of either of them.

In April of 1958, a deserted campsite was discovered on the northern edge of the mountain. A bloodstained blanket, a Geiger counter, a gun cleaning kit (sans gun), cooking utensils and some letters from which the names and address had been torn off were found; but no trace of the occupant was EVER found.

Then, came the 1960s...

In October of 1960 a group of hikers found a headless skeleton near the foot of a cliff on Superstition Mountain. An investigation later determined that it belongs to an Austrian Student by the name of Franz Harrier.

Five days later another skeleton was found; that of William Richard Harvey. The cause of death also unknown.

In January of 1961, a family discovered the body of Hilmer Charles Bohen while picnicking near the edge of the mountain. He was a prospector from Utah who had been shot in the back and his body buried beneath the sand.

In March of that same year, another prospector from Denver was found in Needle Canyon; his name was Walter J Mowry. When his bullet-ridden body was removed to the coroner's, it was ruled a "suicide"

In the autumn of 1961, the police began conducting a search for Jay Clapp; a prospector who had been working on Superstition Mountain for a decade and a half. He had been missing since July and after what was deemed a thorough search, the hunt was called off. Three years later his headless skeleton was finally discovered.

In 1964, Richard and Robert Kremis, two brothers, were found dead at the bottom of a high cliff. That same year, a couple was found murdered in an automobile, parked in almost the same spot.

More similar and unexplained deaths have occurred and continue to occur within these mountains. Jimmy Dale could not seem to impress these facts on her often enough. As much beauty and mystery as the mountains held, they also held great evil.

"Are these many deaths truly part of the old Apache curse? The Devil's Playground, indeed"; thought Elizabeth.

And yet, despite the tragedy, terror, and warnings ... the Superstition's mystery and beauty called to her.

APACHE TEARS

"Dead grass, dry roots, hunger crying in the night

Ghost of broke hearts and laws are here

And who saw the young squaw, they judged by their whiskey

law

Tortured till she died of pain and fear

Where soldiers lay her back, are the black apache tears."

~ Johnny Cash~

Elizabeth knew very little of Indian
customs other than what she gleaned

from the stories told by her old half breed
friend. She had enjoyed the fascinating
histories told by the old man and eagerly
looked forward to evenings spent
camping near the Superstitions with him
and then once he arrived, Ranger too.
Elizabeth would sit around the campfire,
fingering the black obsidian tear drop
that hung from a silver chain around her
neck. It had been a gift from Jimmy Dale
on the first Christmas she was forced to
spend without her precious
granddaughter or Jon. It was called an
Apache Tear drop and other than the
legends he had told her about Creation
and the vortexes of the Superstitions, this
was one of her favorites that she would
ask him to recite to her frequently; not

only for the actual history behind it, but also because of the legend and the magic:

In July of 1870, the Apaches were living life as they always did until General George Stoneman deemed it necessary to establish an outpost" west of what is now called Superior, AZ. Things did not start to get worse for the Indians until the winter, when the tribes began having a difficult time gathering and hunting. The buffalo and vegetation were scarce and the Apache men did not know how they were going to feed their families and tribes. In desperate need of food, the "Pinal Apaches" had made several raids on a settlements.

Unknown to soldiers and settlers alike, a band of Apaches had established an extensive Rancheria on the top of this great rampart of rock, which they reached via a secret pathway, known only to themselves.

From this elevated position, the Indian lookouts were able to obtain an extensive view of the surrounding country and could keep watch of the movements of troops and citizen outfits sent out to punish them.

From means of smoke signals they could also communicate to tribal allies their position, strength and activities of those who would destroy them.

In this camp on the top of Big Picacho,

which was difficult to assault, the Apaches felt comparatively secure from any attack.

The location of this Apache village was suspected, however, due to the fact that, every now and then, a solitary Indian lookout would be seen perched upon the jagged cliffs of the Big Picacho, well out of harm's way, watching the activities at Picket Post just outside of Superior Arizona. But all military attempts to make an effective attack upon them proved futile.

However, after these last raids, the military regulars and some volunteers trailed the tracks of the stolen cattle. Finally, after much tracking and trailing, the secret pathway leading to the Apache encampment was discovered. The Apaches, feeling perfectly safe in their mountain stronghold, had neglected to post lookouts on the trail to warn them of sudden or unexpected danger.

At daybreak, the settlers made a sudden and determined attack upon the surprised and bewildered Apaches, and wrought terrible havoc among them with their first volleys.

The Apaches, confident in the safety of their location, were completely surprised and out-numbered in the attack. Nearly 50 of the band of 75 Apaches were killed in the first volley of shots. The rest of the tribe retreated to the mountain cliff's edge. Without a moment's hesitation, the fleeing warriors threw themselves over the towering cliffs, possibly in the faint hope of escaping fatal injury or perhaps simply because they did not want to be caught and punished by the white man's laws. However, the leap into space was too great and all those warriors (husbands, sons, and brothers) who sought that avenue of escape, were crushed and broken on the rocks below.

For years afterward, those who ventured up the treacherous face of that mountain in AZ found skeletons, or could see the bleached bones wedged in the crevices of the side of the mountain cliffs.

The Apache women and the lovers of those who had died, gathered a short distance from the base of the cliff where the sands were white, and for a month they wept for their dead. They mourned greatly, for they realized that not only had their 75 brave Apache warriors died, but with them had died the great fighting spirit of the Pinal Apaches.

"Legend has it that their sadness was so great, and their burden of sorrow so sincere that Usen imbedded into black stones the tears of the Apache Women who mourned their dead. These black obsidian stones, when held to the light, reveal the translucent tear of the Apache."

"The stones", Jimmy Dale told her, "bring good luck to those possessing them. It is said that whoever owns an Apache Tear will never have to cry again, for the Apache Women have shed their tears in place of yours."

"This, my friend, is what I wish for you"; he had said as he placed the chain about her neck. "You have been crying for those you have loved and lost for far too long."

In gemology, Elizabeth had also learned that black obsidian (Apache Tear) was said to be a powerful Meditation stone. The purpose of this stone was to bring to light that which is hidden from the conscious mind. It dissolves suppressed negative patterns and purifies them. It can create a somewhat radical behavior change as new positive attitudes replace old, negative, egocentric patterns.

Elizabeth now wore this particular stone whenever she went out to hike in her beloved desert or when she was without Jon and felt so terribly alone. Her deep friendship for him had cost her the love of her own children and her precious, precious, granddaughter. It had cost her contact with her grandsons and her youngest granddaughter as well; all out of ignorance and pain and an attempt to control a life that was hers to live. Strange how, when she had met Hunter, her mother, father and sister had turned away from her. Now too, after meeting Jon, her own children had turned away from her.

"Somehow, I am just not meant to be with anyone, I guess. I am not supposed to be happy"; she told herself far too often.

Although wearing the stone did not necessarily stop her tears from flowing, it did remind her that she shared sorrows with other women; brave, strong women, of the Apache tribe. She also hoped it would provide her with positive insight into her own soul which had grown darker since Hunter's passing and blacker still with the estrangement of her children.

But, as always, it was the stories of the Sipapu that captivated Elizabeth the most. One of the most repeated legends was that Indians had come up through the Sipapu in the bottom of the wikiup (Apache house) to inhabit the earth. Indians said they often communicated with the Spirit World through them. She firmly believed in their existence and often told Jimmy Dale that she honestly did feel a pull from time to time, catching a sound of something distant but familiar, or catching a glimpse of someone or something out of the corner of her eye...

Jimmy would look at her silently and nod his head.

Then again there was that soft "tinkling" sound that would whisper in her ear whenever she was out hiking in what she had come to call "her mountain".

In Love with a Desert Mountain Range

"If you don't die of thirst, there are blessings in the desert.
You can be pulled into limitlessness, which we all yearn for,
Or you can do the beauty of minutiae, the scrimshaw of tiny
and precise.
The sky is your ocean, and the crystal silence will uplift you
like great Gospel Music."

The Superstition Mountains were calling
Elizabeth's spirit once again to go and
explore ancient Indian trails and enjoy
the flora and fauna of an ever-changing
landscape. It was the middle of July... the
heat would hit the triple digits today. In
fact, the weather man stated it could
reach 123 degrees; just a little warmer
than the norm for this time of year. It was
also monsoon season when sudden,
unexpected bursts of torrential rains
would suddenly thunder down on desert
dwellers; creating flash floods in some
instances or, if rain did not appear,
massive haboobs (giant sand storms);
some as tall as skyscrapers.

It was during this season that the sweat would rain in sheets down her back while the Thunder God, towering over the upper rocks, numbed her with feverish shadows. A sign of the skies pursuit upon her, as he whispered sage words into her ears, while his rough sandpapered hands tried to kill her and anyone else who dared to enter his land during this season.

Still, she had been out in this weather before (despite friendly warnings), and the chance of spending time out in the Superstitions during **just such a storm** would prove even more interesting and exhilarating as she consistently searched for the mysterious vortexes so often spoken of in various legends and stories of the mystical mountain range. *As she consistently searched for answers to her damaged soul and life*

Elizabeth stood only 5' 2" tall and, although blonde haired and blue eyed, was actually 1/2 American Indian; it was her German half that apparently held the dominant gene in her as opposed to her brothers and sisters who were all dark haired. However, the shape of her eyes and face, the high cheek bones, the long thick hair and her, as yet, fairly unwrinkled face, were a tribute to that Indian heritage. Her tribe was actually the Tuscarora (the tribe that eventually settled in the New York area) and although she had studied the history and the lineage of that proud segment of the Iroquois Nation, her absolute fascination was with the Apache nation; its history and its beautiful people.

True, Arizona's Superstition Mountains had long been the source of stories about lost gold; those legends of the Dutchman's Lost Gold Mine, Jesuit treasure, Peralta gold and numerous other lost gold mine stories, which still attract men and women from far and near to this rugged mountain range east of Apache Junction. However, it was always the history of the Apache that drew Elizabeth there and not the allure or promise of hidden gold.

The first time Liz had approached the Superstitions she thought she was seeing an ancient stone fortress... Looking at it as she and a friend were driving toward Tucson on the 60, she remembered rubbing the sweat from her eyes but the image did not go away. Then as the car approached closer, she began to question her own eyes and state of mind as the rocks began to take on yet other forms of imagery; and she began to see ancient gods, and dragon Lords...mythical creatures and more.

The images began to morph and her mind was spinning as she heard and felt within her mind the understandings of another time, a time when ancient spirits walked this earth. For Elizabeth, it was a time when magic and Shamanic reality intertwined with the dominant consciousness of this Desert of the Universe.

She would spend hours hiking along trails like the Peralta or those leading to

Weaver's Needle looking for artifacts and feeling the almost electrical charge that would suddenly come into the early morning or late night air. It was said that Don Miguel Peralta, discovered a vein of

rich gold while searching for the treasure described to Coronado, "where the peak, or spire, looked more like a finger pointing upwards, or the ""Finger of God."" Paulino Weaver later used the rock as a place to etch his name with a knife and subsequent prospectors discovered the etching and dubbed the landmark "Weaver's Needle"."

Hiking these areas, Elizabeth would dodge the expanse which chokes the forearm of the Weaver's needle looming behind the "Devil of Superstition Mountain", who, according to the stories of Jimmy Dale, stole both Pima and Apache children and maidens. Jimmy Dale told her not to tempt fate. Apparently, they believed the path became "Satan's Trickster"; standing with his mouth agape and swallowing them with the rising altitude – full fisting the landscape. Territorial asylum of the hunted.

"One day, though", she thought to herself, "I will HAVE to enter that trail... I know I will; one way or another."

So, today, she put together her backpack for a long day hike, ensured her survival needs were all in place (from bobcat/coyote attack, to snake bite, to sun burn, to bee sting), strapped on extra water along with her canteen, grabbed her light long sleeved shirt, her survival knife, and her whistle. She then strapped on her holster and secured her 38 Smith and Wesson Revolver. Finally, she put her medicine bag around her neck that carried corn meal and a crystal from the mountain. Jimmy Dale had given this to her several years ago to help appease the angry spirits of the Mountain should she encounter them. Then she picked up her shepherd pup's leash.

She had adopted her furry companion about two months ago, shortly after she had been laid off from yet another contract position. (Working contract positions had been hard since her layoff from the phone company a few years ago, but it paid the bills.) She named him Ranger. From the very start, he loved to go hiking. Still every inch a puppy, he was curious, mischievous, filled with energy and love, and sometimes VERY destructive. She often felt she had to tell him "No" far too much, but her trainer said that a German shepherd required love, exercise, a job to do and **lots** of discipline. He definitely kept her busy on all of those fronts. He was an excellent companion on her long hikes, which she took almost daily in her search for not only knowledge of the mysteries of the Superstition, so rich in Native American and early pioneer history, but for the peace and serenity she found there. It was here that her writer's muse also came to life and inspiration flowed. Two books of poetry had already found their inspiration from this mountain range; more were sure to follow.

Elizabeth whistled -- well, as best as she could whistle -- which often sounded like someone who had been eating very dry crackers and needed a good long drink. But her pup's satellite dish ears (which had just started standing erect last month) heard her every time as he clumsily came running across the slick tile floor, all four paws slipping and sliding until he skidded to a stop right in front of her. His head tilting first to the left and then to the right and back again, deep almond eyes, sparkling, and an overly long tail swishing back and forth furiously; he anxiously waited for what his mistress was going to say.

"Wanna go hiking boy?" she asked. It really was a silly question as NOTHING made this puppy happier than getting in the jeep, sticking his head out the window and heading out to the desert. There was so much obedience training she had yet to do with him, but his intelligent eyes, that long brown nose, those gigantic bat winged ears and the whimsical head tilt made it very hard for her to make him behave. Suddenly, in response to her question, he jumped up on her, paws firmly on her chest, knocking her back against the wall.

"No!" she laughingly scolded him. "That's a bad puppy!" "No!"

The pup looked down at his overly large feet on his quickly growing long legs as if to say "I am sorry". She reached down to pet him and he leaned into her, raising up his one front paw to give her his version of a shepherd hug. Elizabeth laughed, clipped the leash to his collar, gave a gentle tug and said "Let's go!"

As they started to head out the front door, she suddenly remembered that she had forgotten something. "Ooops boy, we almost forgot the water bowl that Jon bought for you for our trips out to the desert and your treats. We have to have treats for those times when you are a good dog, don't we boy?"

Giving him the "down-stay" command, he lay down by the door and patiently waited for her; his head tilting from one side to the other as he watched.

She went back into the kitchen, reached on top of the refrigerator into the basket that held the shepherd pup's treats and grabbed a bag of his favorite; sweet potato and salmon, and the collapsible water bowl which she clipped to her belt. This water bowl had been a great find and gift from Jon as she was still unable to teach Ranger to drink from a bottle. Made of water proof canvas and lined with a plastic liner, it folded up in to a small case that could be carried on her belt. When needed, she simply unzipped it and it became a bowl she could fill with water. Grabbing up the leash, they went out the front door, walked through the patio gate and headed toward the Jeep.

"NO" and the Writer's Life

It's always seemed as though pets attach themselves
to writers (and vice versa, of course) in greater numbers
than to regular folks. Maybe it's the pull of a constant,
silent listener to bounce ideas against,

or the boundless soul of the writer.

Elizabeth had lost her beloved husband to drug addiction and heart disease, but prior to losing him and her move out to Arizona, she had always owned cats and Shihtzus for pets. Her work, family, and writing obligations did not permit much time to socialize or to be outside as she would have loved to have been, so these types of pets were more conducive to her lifestyle. Additionally, living on the Texas Gulf Coast with its high humidity, and heat, as well as her absolute dislike for ocean beaches, kept her inside most of the time anyway. Elizabeth had grown up with dogs as a child, cocker spaniels, and loved them dearly, but she always felt that a "real" dog (medium to large breed) was not conducive to a writer's lifestyle.

However, after her husband's death and a long six years of loneliness, during which time she continued to help her now grown children as much as possible and assisted in raising her precious granddaughter for over 10 years, she had found a new "soul mate" named Jon, who encouraged her to return to her love of hiking, her love of the mountains and desert, her love of travel and her love of writing. Although Jon had always been extremely tender with her two very old Shihtzus, Taffy and Isis (who had been born blind), she could sense how much he, as a "red blooded male", yearned for a "real" dog. She had learned that, as a young boy, Jon's father, in an absolute act of alcoholic rage and cruelty, had shot the only dog he had ever owned. It was not until the death of her beloved Isis that she opted to get such a "real dog". She decided upon a German shepherd as she was told they made great hiking companions, were definitely a "man's dog", **and** her late husband had owned a beautiful Belgian Shepherd named Sarge when they first met. It felt like the right breed to adopt and one that just might fit the lifestyle she now embraced so fully; well except for that damned writing part.

Ignoring all the best advice and forgetting the history of the direct association between cats and writers, she went headlong into her pet adoption project and Ranger, the exuberant German shepherd puppy, entered her life in the late spring of 2012. So it is clear that

Elizabeth had to make a sad admission; she could not be a *real* writer at all as she chose to have a large dog as a pet.

Now there was of course the initial period in their relationship of leash and "potty" training and a getting to know the "personality" that followed as little Ranger was clearly trying his very best to fit in with her quiet and concentrated writer's lifestyle; which was proving not quite so successful! He was a mischievous and destructive pup!

Elizabeth even happily pled forgiveness for him when, upon returning from her new job, she found him he munching away happily on a book she had just received from a writer friend; Dr. Joseph

Ocean. The cover was beyond saving, but luckily his taste in words kept him from eating the text and that was the truly valuable part of the book; right? So, although she scolded him, she was immediately down on her knees cuddling with him and getting very sloppy I'm sorry kisses.

Then came the rapid series of events in late spring and early summer that started to give her reason to understand why cats or small breed dogs have been the pet of choice for writers over the eons.

Event One: Neither cats nor Shihtzus habitually reduce pencils to a thousand splinters in 30 seconds. Ranger not only reduced wooden pencils into splinters but did it with any mechanical pencil or pen she left out on her desk, counters, or tables as well.

"No! No! No!" Elizabeth would yell.

Ranger would sit down on his haunches, tilt his head to one side and look as if he were saying "What?", then walk over to her and lick her face. Needless to say, Elizabeth would melt, get down on her knees and hug her silly puppy.

Event Two: Neither cats nor Shihtzus can imaginatively turn 125 pages of printed work documents, needed to give to Field Engineers the following day, into a raging snow storm. (And people wonder why they nicknamed this breed "the German

Shredder.") Coming through the door for a quick bite of lunch before going back to the office, Elizabeth had found this exact snow storm of a disaster. Elizabeth had sunk to the ground crying and yelling "No! No! No!", while the bewildered pup slumped to the ground whining; so unsure of what he had done wrong.

There was now no time for lunch as she spent the time cleaning up the house, reprimanding Ranger, and repairing her makeup after crying from the frustration and Ranger licking her face. Yep, all was forgiven before she went back to the office. It always was. How she loved that dog.

Event Three: Neither cats or Shihtzus have an ongoing and totally ingrained habit of slapping huge (often wet) paws on your keyboard at least 4 times a day, or coming up and shoving their cold wet nose right into your face/mouth/eye, in an unmistakable sign that a walk or ball play is an absolute imperative within the next 30 seconds; or else! If ignored, there were dangerous consequences involving electrical cables and the power supply to the much needed PC. Saying "no!" here would do absolutely NO good whatsoever. What Ranger wanted; Ranger got and it made no difference if she was inspired by the muses or not. Ranger came first!

Event Four: Neither cats nor Shihtzus have ever been known to consume the first printed proof copy of your new book. Now Elizabeth knew that her shepherd was extremely intelligent and clever, but she had the distinct feeling he didn't really understand all of the 254 plus pages of words he had shredded in one sitting.

Her favorite pen, an eagle feather attached to a pen nub and blessed by a Lakota Medicine Man, had also been included in this episode; dessert she presumed.

This was nearly the straw that broke an old camel's back... as the pen had been with Elizabeth for over 30 years and was her "good luck" charm when it came to her writing. It had sat on writing desks in her various homes over the years and never been touched; not by ferrets, birds, cats, Shihtzus, Rottweilers, or squirrels that had run freely through her home throughout those years. Ranger had done the unthinkable!

She dissolved into tears sobbing loudly "No! No! No! Why? why? You have all kinds of toys? Why? You bad boy!"

This time a sad, guilty puppy seemed to know he had done something VERY bad as he belly crawled up to her, put his head in her lap and whined piteously right along with her until she looked down at his pathetic form, stopped crying, and began petting and comforting him.

"Silly, silly dog. I can't stay mad at you"

Event Five: Cats and even Shihtzus, of course, can usually be accommodated in the writing process; sitting on your lap, purring or snoring away while a writer happily does his or her own purring, but hopefully NOT snoring, on a keyboard. With a German shepherd this is not so easy. However, on a couple of occasions, this shepherd pup had definitely managed to type out a few things he wanted to say while sitting beside Elizabeth with his chin often resting on the desk top as if waiting for his turn to type. He generally managed to do so when she took a break to get more coffee and often left cryptic messages for her on the computer screen.

"*Qwebnm,.qwertjkl;' "* was one of the last messages he had left for her. Problem was, Elizabeth still had not learned to speak fluent dog. Ranger sure made her want to learn how though, as she felt he definitely had something to say.

Event Six: Apparently Ranger DEEPLY resented any time Liz spent watching television. Now, she did not have a great deal of time to do so but did have specific old movies or family shows she liked to watch when time would allow. The only time he did not seem to object was when she watched the movie "K-9" starring Jim Belushi. Then he would sit beside her chair and watch the movie with her. However, one morning, when she went to reach for the television remote control, she found it missing. Several hours later, she finally found it. He had attempted to bury it in the back yard. He had gotten his way for a few hours... no TV that day!

She had taken Ranger out to the Superstitions for his very first hike when he was only 8 weeks old (two weeks after bringing him home). Funny, he had been born in the shadow of that beautiful mountain range and now would be spending much of his growing years wandering it with Elizabeth. How small he looked riding in the front seat beside her all the way down to the mountain. He was also VERY inquisitive and already showing himself to be very loyal.

Elizabeth had talked to him all the way down to the mountain, reminding him of how much fun they would have, but how important that it was for him to be a good - good dog.

"There are scores of openings, caves and crevices through-out the mountainous terrain. There are also many critters such as rattlesnakes, scorpions, bobcat, and coyotes (wild dogs like you) that you don't want an encounter with. Why even the cacti can be quite painful if you get too close! So you need to listen... okay. "

Ranger tilted his head and barked and vocalized as if telling her "silly woman, surely you can see I am too excited to listen".

Immediately after getting out of the Jeep, Ranger went straight towards a jumping Cholla and nearly got it stuck in his little black nose.

"NO!" Shouted Elizabeth. "No!"

Ranger looked down dejectedly which made Elizabeth regret her angry words, reach down, and pet him. Off he shot...

exploring the beautiful Superstitions. He would only get a few feet in front of her though before he would look back as if to say "are you okay"? Or, "is it all right to keep going"?

Suddenly she saw him tense and draw one foot up as he stared down at the ground. He had found a small snake. Elizabeth determined right away that it was not poisonous and allowed him to follow his instincts. Slowly he crept up on it and as he went to nudge it with his nose the snake slithered off in another direction. Ranger jumped about 5 feet back in temporary surprise and then was in hot pursuit. He followed it up to a dead bush and then the snake protectively

coiled itself, which for some reason made
Ranger think it was time to end the chase.

He was off again, sure footedly heading up
the mountain trail, exploring everything.
He even chased a jack rabbit or two, but
Elizabeth was certain that Ranger felt
they were 'relatives' and that he wanted
to have a family reunion. It's the ears
don't you know.

The hikes became more frequent and
Ranger was growing rapidly, but
remained the ever the mischievous puppy
forever being told "NO" ,and sometimes
by a very over tired and impatient
Elizabeth who would then see the results
of her anger on this gentle loving spirit
and regret every minute of it.

When they were inside their home and Elizabeth would reprimand Ranger by saying "No! Go to bed" Ranger would slowly walk over to his bed, look over at her to make sure she was watching, and then pick it up in his mouth and throw it as if to say "but I hate my bed". He loved his sticks and his ball but he hated his bed; unless it was bedtime.

So after hundreds of these little episodes, do you think she wanted to do a swap for a cat or Shihtzus? Not in a million years. Today, Elizabeth just couldn't imagine writing uninterrupted ever again. Her time with her new best friend was too valuable. And anyway, she needed more time to think and all this walking really

helped to break up her day and break
through the writer's block. Add this to the
fact that he had become quite the hiker,
her sole companion for at least six
months out of every year, and her best
friend. She knew she could depend on his
unconditional love no matter what. He
was with her when she woke up every
morning and the last thing she saw before
she went to sleep. Ranger had become
Elizabeth's only "family".

However, despite the fact that a
beautifully engraved tag, with military
designs (in honor of her husband's and
Jon's military service), hung from the red
collar around her puppy's neck, proudly
displaying the name "Ranger" on it,
Elizabeth was quite certain that her dog

felt his name was NO! He heard that word said to him far more often than he did his name and sometimes she wondered if it "wounded" his soul in any way.

Yes, soul! How could anyone look into the eyes of a dog and NOT see that he had a soul? "A spirit purer than any human's", Elizabeth conjectured. She often thought of him (and her previous dogs) as a guardian angel.

Elizabeth opened up the back door on the driver's side of the Jeep and the young shepherd leaped inside, knowing full well he was going to spend a day freely roaming the desert and mountain with his human. She ensured he was safely in before rolling down the back windows just enough so he could stick his head out to catch the wind in his large ears and visit with people who pulled up alongside during the 30 minute plus drive out toward Apache Junction. He always attracted attention, which he loved (and so did she). He was a handsome dog, her Ranger.

GOLDFIELD AND ITS
HAUNTED MINE

"There is a road in the hearts of all of us, hidden and
seldom traveled
Which leads to an unknown, secret place..."
~Chief Luther Standing Bear~

To get to the Superstition mountains, at
least to this particular section that she felt
certain would eventually lead her to a
Sipapu and a vortex to another place,
time, or dimension, she would head down

Main Street in Mesa, Arizona which would
eventually turn in to Apache Trail. The
Apache Trail was once an old stagecoach
trail that ran through the Superstitions. It
was named the Apache Trail after
the Apache Indians who originally used
this trail to move through the mountains.

The Apache trail, (the northeastern end),
runs through the Superstition Mountains
and the Tonto National Forest. Today,
much of the Apache Trail is paved, and
the section east of Apache Junction is
known officially as State Route 88. It is
also the main traffic corridor through
Apache Junction, turning into Main Street
as the road passes into Mesa, and regains
the Apache name once more by becoming
Apache Boulevard in Tempe, ending at

Mill Avenue and college town. Prior to the completion of the Superstition Freeway in 2002, the Apache Junction portion of the Apache Trail was part of US Highway 60, which was rerouted to the Superstition Freeway once it was completed. Unfortunately, slowly but surely, urbanization is creeping up on this ancient and beautiful land.

Elizabeth loved the fact that the Apache and Yavapai used the trail, not only for their infamous predatory raids against the Pima along the Salt and Gila Rivers south and west of the Superstition Mountains, but also for daily travel. The Apache and Yavapai continued their raids after the arrival of the Anglo-Americans in the early 1850s. The Army quelled (a polite name for destroyed) the so-called predatory Apache-Yavapai in this region by 1868. There were other military campaigns fought against renegade Apaches from 1871 until Geronimo's surrender in 1886 at Skeleton Canyon in Southern Arizona. This was where Elizabeth eventually hoped to wind up on today's outing

Loving the countryside around her, she generally veered away from the 60 and the newly built 202, and turned right onto Main street, pushed "CD" on the Jeep's stereo and began singing along with America;

""""...in the desert, you can't remember your name cause their ain't no one for to give you no pain..."""" Oh how right you were you old band you... out in the desert, no one can hurt me..." Ranger did his best to sing along, howling away right along with her.

Today, as she always did when heading to the mountains; she would drive through the small town of Apache Junction which lies 33 degrees parallel to the Devil's triangle. (Elizabeth loved to tell people about the "Devil's Triangle" as she loved the looks on their faces). She would then pass by one of her favorite little tourist traps, The Goldfield Haunted Mine, where she had spent many happy hours with Jon and with her sweet granddaughter. Inwardly she repeated to herself...
"Someday I will live out here... as close as I

can get to that beautiful, magical

mountain range."

Situated atop a small hill between the Superstition Mountains and the Goldfield Mountains, the settlement of Goldfield got its start in 1892 when a very rich, high grade gold ore was found in the area. A town soon sprang up and on October 7, 1893 it received its first official post office.

This "official" find, coupled with the legend of the Lost Dutchman Mine, which had been circulating for years, led plenty of new miners to the area and in no time the town boasted three saloons, a boarding house, a general store, a brewery, a blacksmith shop, a butcher shop, and a school. For five years the town boomed until some 1,500 people were residing in the burgeoning city. But just as with other gold camps, Goldfield's bustling days were quickly dashed when the vein of gold ore started to play out and the grade of the ore dropped even more. Just five years after it began, the town found itself quickly dying. The miners moved on, the post office was discontinued on November 2, 1898, and Goldfield became a ghost town.

However, some prospectors clung on to the area, determined to find the elusive Lost Dutchman Mine or perhaps, a brand new vein. Others tried to reopen the existing mines, but all attempts were unsuccessful until a man named George Young, who was then the secretary of

Arizona and the acting governor, arrived on the scene in the 1900s.

Young brought in new mining methods and equipment to recover the ore and the town slowly began to come alive once again. During this time, they also built a mill and a cyanide plant. A second post office was established on June 8, 1921

and the "new" town was called
Youngberg. However, the town's
"rebirth" would last only about as long as
it did the first time around – just five
years. Finally, the gold vein was
exhausted, the post office was
discontinued on October 30, 1926, and
the town died a second time.

Goldfield was obviously not destined to
die permanently, though. In 1966, Robert
F. Schoose, a long time ghost town,
mining, and treasure-hunting enthusiast,
made his first trip to the Superstition
Mountains and instantly fell in love with
the area. (Elizabeth could not blame him;
she had done the exact same thing.) He
moved to Mesa, Arizona in 1970 and soon
began to dream of owning his own ghost

town. He had heard of the old site of Goldfield, but upon inspection, he found little left other than a few foundations and rambling shacks. He then located another five-acre site that was once the location of the Goldfield Mill and decided to rebuild the old town.

Purchasing the old mill site in 1984, they first reconstructed a mining tunnel, which included a snack bar, and opened for business in 1988. Next came a photo shop, the Blue Nugget, a General Store, the Mammoth Saloon and the Goldfield Museum.

Today, Goldfield is filled with authentic looking buildings, includes underground mine tours, and the only narrow gauge

railroad in operation in Arizona.
Numerous shops and buildings include a
haunted brothel, bakery, leather works, a
jail, livery, and more. The authentic
looking street is filled with people in
period costume, horses and wagons, and
sometimes authentic gunfighter
presentations.

Most people who visit Arizona love
Tombstone for its authenticity, but
Elizabeth loved Goldfield even more;
primarily because she could walk the
main street or eat at the Saloon and gaze
at her beloved Superstition whenever the
mood hit her.

However, she would not be going to the
Lost Dutchman State Park today, which

had become far too over run with yuppies, Millennials, and unruly teenagers who were slowly destroying the calm quiet beauty of the desert; not only with the trash they left behind but with their music and non-stop talking. Nor would she be stopping in at Goldfield. No, today, she was heading out towards the back side of Peralta trail and the "darker" side of the Superstitions. She was seeking peace, solitude, and wonder against Jimmy Dale's well intentioned advice.

"Someday", Elizabeth said out loud to her furry companion, "we **will** live out here. Someday... I promise, Ranger" She said EVERY time she got close to the mountains.

It was true that, ever since the death of her husband, and the beginning of her relationship with a new found love who had taught her to drive and showed her the beauty of the desert, she only felt truly at peace there. There was a special form of spiritual connection between her soul and the desert... and the Superstitions were akin to a cathedral to her.

She had experienced a similar experience in Sedona years before when first her oldest son and then her daughter were married at Cathedral Rock in simple but such beautiful out door ceremonies; both brides breathtakingly beautiful against the setting of the Red Rock.

It was there, in 2006, that she had
released the ashes of her first love with
their youngest son at her side. As she did,
a red tailed hawk had flown over head
and as they were leaving, even though it
was nearing October, a lone butterfly had
landed on a single wild flower just in front
of her; she knew Hunter was at peace.
However, there was no peace in her soul;
just questions, and sadness and loss.

ARRIVING

"...The summit of the mountain,
The thunder of the sky,
The Rhythm of the waters, speaks to me...
And my heart soars."
~Chief Dan George~

It was a Cinerama morning, not unlike
millions of other days that had begun
with spreading tangerine/peach/rose
across the same turquoise sky and golden
rays on that very desert floor, for eons
past. Somehow she always found it

comforting to know that she was walking with the ancients.

It was a morning Liz often described as a water color morning; with variegated rainbow hues of light in the east against a pacific blue background. As always, the Superstitions were ever changing.

She had decided to hike a rather strenuous area today, one that would allow her to climb higher and also descend down into seldom traversed canyons; her hike today would be along the Lower Rogers Canyon Trail.

At its height she would reach almost 1500 feet and could possibly travel a total of 15.8 miles, should she so desire. It would also allow her to access areas closer to the Weaver's Needle and, she had been told, some fantastic Indian Ruins. This was a place, Jimmy Dale had said, where some swore they heard the distinct sound of distant drums and a few travelers had never returned.

A few drops of early moisture on a lone cactus at Elizabeth's feet, waiting to vanish as the sun would spread more warmth across the landscape, caught her thoughts for a moment as she stepped down from the Jeep. In the kaleidoscope reflection, she swore she caught a familiar face. Overhead, a red tailed hawk called out its greeting.

Opening up the back door, out jumped a playful, excited shepherd who immediately started to chase a small lizard.

"No!" reprimanded Elizabeth. "No, No, No!. Now you know better than that!"

She gave a firm tug on his leash, pulled him over to her side, and seeing the sad look on his face, rubbed his head and let him nuzzle her cheek. How she loved this sweet pup.

There had been a small rain storm in the very early hours that day, and you could still smell the wetness in the air...

"Monsoon season is here, boy"; Elizabeth said to her dog. We have to be wary not to be trapped by one if we are down in the one of the canyons here."

Ranger barked twice as if agreeing with her statement and then saw something that just had to be investigated.

Looking down she saw that the pup was totally oblivious to her warnings or her teachings and was now digging up the cactus flower she had just moments ago been admiring.

"No!" she admonished the dog. "That's bad. No! Sit!"

Ranger sat down, looking dejected. It was such a pretty flower and it tasted so sweet. He did not like making her tense and sad. This was his human and he loved her so -- but everything was so fascinating and wonderful!

Gathering the rest of her hiking things from the back of the truck, she donned the backpack, placed her hiking belt on (which held things of immediate need such as water, a whistle, and her knife), around her waist, gave a gentle tug on the leash and said "Let's go boy, there is a lot for us to see and do before the sun gets high in the sky."

Off in the distance, well beyond the Phoenix sky line, she saw clouds forming;

but for now the sun shone brightly on the mountain.

THE DESERT ANGEL

"The Red Tailed Hawk represents all Hawks and carries all their individual strengths and knowledge. Its medicine empowers a person to seek out their ancestral roots and to examine in depth that which is positive so that it may be integrated into the person's life and that which is limiting so it can be released. Tradition is only worth honoring when it supports joy and fulfillment in one's life! In this tradition, Hawk also helps a person to move forward in life and to seek out great quests to embark upon.

The sky is Hawk's realm, and through its flight it communicates with Heaven and the Great Creator Spirit, and conveys that knowledge to earth: Hawk medicine unites Heaven and Earth. This powerful bird can awaken the visionary within you, and lead to your life purpose. It is the Messenger, and when it shows up pay attention: there is always a message coming. Hawk helps us to not only be aware that we are receiving a message but how to interpret it. The realm of symbols is also the realm of Hawk for Hawk is able to soar high above the earth to soar on the breath of Spirit, to commune with Spirit and thus understand through the intuitive level what the message means and what can be done to move forward in life."

Elizabeth looked up at the still gorgeous turquoise blue sky, scattered with a grey cloud here and there, and made a mental note of the ever circling red-tail hawk drifting majestically overhead.

At times, she wondered to herself if there really were only one or two of these beautiful birds on the entire planet. Since her arrival in AZ, it seemed that everywhere she went there would be one red-tailed hawk doing its graceful, gliding ballet of freedom. She often thought that it might be the same one – the same one that had flown over head as she had released her beloved Hunter's ashes into the river at Oak Creek Canyon so many years ago.

Of course, Elizabeth KNEW better (her logic and intellect truly were intact) but, somehow, it always made her feel like she had her own private angel that could see all and know all. A spiritual entity, in physical form, undaunted and untouched

by humankind's arrogance and stupidity,
that would lead her to a better way and
watch over her; if only she would follow...

THE STORM

"Terrified by the "Thunder God's
Illuminating wrath
On who's sacred ground we trespassed"

The Native Americans believed that the
monsoon winds were the souls of people
from the "Otherworld", which was located
beneath the Superstition Mountains.
With torrential rains, high speed winds,
and monstrous dust storms the monsoon
was Elizabeth desert version of the "Wild
Hunt" (a supernatural force that sweeps

across the land at night. The actual object of the Hunt varies from place to place. In some areas it searches for anything that might be unfortunate enough to be in its path.)

Maybe it was because she knew what time of year was fast approaching, that the past was also coming up for air all more frequently than usual for Elizabeth. She still mourned the loss of her first love who had left this world over 18 years ago, during monsoon season, and still longed to be with him. Perhaps the monsoon winds really were the voices of those just beyond that thin veil of the here and now. Perhaps one of those voices was Hunter's or her recently deceased mother? Elizabeth only knew that it was creating horrible nightmares for her, often involving her late husband, her mother, Ranger, or Jon. Several times over the course of the past several weeks her own screams had woken her from deep sleeps and she would be calling out Jon's name or Ranger's as she woke. One such night, Ranger broke through the barrier gate to the upstairs to reach her, jumped into the queen sized bed, and nuzzled her for the rest of the night. It was one of the few times she did not say "No!" or scold him for getting on the furniture. She so welcomed his companionship and love that night; she needed it so.

Funny thing is, as terrifying as they were, she could never remember any detail in these dreams; only that there was intense fear and loss involved. She wanted answers and firmly believed the Superstitions held them. She thought about her adoptive mother, Mary, who had died in last autumn, alone and sick... Mary was always afraid of Elizabeth's dreams which had made Elizabeth keep most of them to herself.

"Truth is, Mom", Elizabeth whispered out loud, "I think you were just plain afraid of **me**. Between the dreams, the epilepsy, and my ""big words"", you always thought I was so strange. I think, maybe, you were right..."

She still could not shed the guilt she felt over not being with her mother in her final years; but she also could not help but remember how she was kept at arm's length or her mother telling her, right after Hunter had died, that she could come home but not the kids. How her mother had hated Hunter!

The rip in Elizabeth's soul was deeper than the canyons of the Superstitions.

Elizabeth and Ranger hiked for hours, occasionally stopping to take photographs with her cell phone of the various rock formations, cacti, and wildlife or to grab a bite to eat from the rations she carried in her backpack of fruit (apples and raisins), jerky, string cheese (dog treats galore) and M&M's (for Liz only), and always to take long drinks. The further up the trail they progressed, the more difficult the climb became and the more frequently she would stop to let Ranger and her catch their breath.

As there had been no fellow hikers on this path, which is exactly what she was hoping and had planned for, Elizabeth had removed Ranger's leash so he could roam freely. Periodically, she would also check the condition of the pads on his paws to ensure they were not being torn by rocks along the hike. (Should that begin to happen she had special booties to put on him and they would turn around immediately and head for home.) Before long, they were clambering over boulders larger than fully grown men. Elizabeth, now nearing 60, had to take more time to climb over these massive rocks that had been thrown by the mountains during volcanic eruptions centuries before. Ranger, on the other hand, leaped across them like a gazelle, but always only went just so far away from her, turned to watch, and waited patiently for her to catch up.

Elizabeth stopped to catch her breath after pulling herself up on a fairly large rock and suddenly noticed the massive anvil-shaped thunderhead clouds that were forming in the distance; quickly closing in on the Superstitions. Looking down toward the place where she had left the Jeep (hours and miles ago) and then at her watch, she knew there would not be time to get back down the mountain and to the Jeep before the storm hit; she had to get herself and her pup out of the weather before the deluge hit.

According to legend and myth the great "Thunder God" of the Apache roars during the summer months in Arizona. Many of us do not find this hard to believe if we have experienced a severe and violent desert thunderstorm during the summer monsoon season. The lightning, thunder and winds will convince any nonbeliever that these storms can be dangerous and violent. Elizabeth fingered the medicine bag hanging from her neck and it calmed her.

Now, scientifically speaking, we know that lightning can be caused by the attraction of unlike electrical charges within a large storm cell. The rapid movement of ice and water molecules, going up and down in a thunderhead cell, creates friction that results in enormous amounts of static electricity being produced. A single lightning discharge can produce about 30 million volts at 125,000 amperes. A discharge can occur in less than 1/10 of a second. The results of a lightning strike can be horrific and very few people survive being struck.

Also, the rapid rising and falling of warm and cold moist air also creates violent bursts of energy. This type of storm activity can result in microburst. Microburst can develop winds that momentarily reach up to 200 mph. As the clouds build and combine, they form massive anvil-shaped thunderheads clouds. These clouds are massive static generators dispersing lightning and creating violent winds. These summer storms can be extremely dangerous and destructive. It is these giant thunderheads that dominate the sky above the Superstition Mountain during the monsoon season and the lightning produced by these storms over the mountains can be spectacular.

If you've ever witnessed an electrical storm over the Superstition Mountains, and Elizabeth had on several occasions as well as the storms of dust called haboob, it is not difficult to see why the early Native Americans held the mountain in such awe. While we can partially explain the phenomena today with modern science, the Indians could only look to their religious shaman for an explanation. It certainly was their "Thunder God" with all his fury.

Elizabeth knew that even modern man, with all of this science and technological know-how should also respect the awesome power of their "Thunder God."

Looking up at the pinnacles of stone, which can now be seen projecting from the summit of one of the peaks of the Superstition Mountains, she remembered the tail of the "stone people":

"Indian legend has it that the Great Spirit, angry over the behavior of the people, stuck his staff into the ground to cause a great flood, and water covered the earth. Most of the people perished, but some escaped and followed a shaman known as White Feather, who fled to the top of Superstition Mountains. The water rose, covering all the valley until it was as high as the line of white sandstone, which is a conspicuous

182

landmark. White Feather, surrounded by his followers, tried all his magic in vain to prevent the further rise of the flood. When he saw he was powerless to prevent this, he gathered all his people and consulted them, saying, "I have exhausted all magic powers but one, which I will now try." Taking in his left hand a medicine stone from his pouch, he held it at arm's length, at the same time extending his right hand toward the sky. After he had sung four songs he raised his hand and seized the lightning and with it struck the stone which he held. This broke into splinters with a peal of thunder and all his people were transformed into the pinnacles of stone. It is said they now stand watch over all who need protection."

Hopefully, these stone people were now watching over Elizabeth and her pup. She took a pinch of corn meal and sprinkled it around her hoping to appease the mountain spirits and gain their favor.

They continued to hike upwards - Elizabeth kept reassuring herself that it was the right way to go as she did not want to be in a canyon or wash when the storm hit, and felt the trust and love coming back to her from her pup. After what felt like hours of scrabbling through bushes and clambering over rocks, however, Elizabeth started to cry; more from fatigue and frustration than anything else. In the back of her mind she heard Jimmy Dale's words of warning.

"I'm sorry," she said to Ranger as she reached down to pet him, "I'll get us out of this. I promise"

She had no real idea how, but she knew she had to keep him safe; she loved him so. She had come to rely on this sweet dog for comfort and love when the world had become so harsh and unbending.

Sitting on the cloud split peak, a vulture observed the pair, bloody-eyed and gall-footed with hungered tenacity; their route ascended beneath it. In her mind, sandstone volcanic pinnacles appeared to charge forward like ancient American soldiers, while the war whoop of Indians and a hawk cried overhead; definite signs of exposure and fatigue.

Elizabeth felt as though she and Ranger were spinning in circles. Her body felt on fire with every step. Every twist was like a knife cutting through a maze of dead body undergrowth, with boulders on stones broken like tomahawk heads. The "eye" of the needle was compelling her, a large eroded eyelet rock, swirling in a mesmerism of kaleidoscope colors.

Night was falling and they had been walking for hours. The winds had picked up greatly and lightening was flashing in the distance-- growing closer, and droplets of rain hit the ground from time to time.

In the distance, Elizabeth could see an overhanging rock and what appeared to be a cave. This was where Elizabeth was sure they would find shelter so she decided to head in that direction. She felt a lot calmer having a safe destination to head towards- until she came to a steep rock face made up of a series of small ledges; the only route up to that cave. The path seemed precarious at best, but Elizabeth was convinced that she and her dog could somehow hop down from ledge to ledge; well she had no doubt that her sure footed shepherd could.

Kneeling down beside Ranger, she gave him a long drink and a treat. Petting him and then hugging him tightly, she pointed to the cave entrance and gave him the command; "Go boy!"

Licking her face, the agile shepherd obeyed and began leaping up the ledges toward the cave.

Shouldering her back pack, taking a deep breath, and whispering a prayer, with the Thunder god shouting his warning in her ears, Elizabeth began the precarious climb to what she hoped was safety...

THE FALL

"Oh Great Spirit, whose voice I hear in the wind
I come to you as one of your many children
I need your strength and your wisdom
Make me strong, not to be superior to my brother,
But to be able to fight my greatest enemy
Myself"
~Chief Dan George~`

Elizabeth had one foot wedged in a crack and the other trying to find a foothold when she felt herself losing her balance. She reached forward to grasp a boulder on which to steady herself only to feel it crumble in her hand and knew she was falling.

There is no way to explain the sickening sounds or feelings of one's own bones being shattered as your body crashes down a mountain side like a rag doll. Strange, she would remember later, that she really had felt little to nothing at the moment of impact. But she remembered hearing her own head crack like a pumpkin and feeling like she had been falling for hours, when in fact only minutes had passed.

She fell down the jagged face of the mountain- more than 25 feet - crashing against abutted rocks as she went. Then she just lay on her back with her legs crushed beneath her, looking up at the mountain top and seeing Ranger, standing at the entrance to the cave looking down - - and the vulture... Then, everything went gray.

Regaining consciousness, she could hear her dog's frantic howls and whines.

"I'm here, I'm fine," she tried to say, but nothing came out. She knew she was not fine, not fine at all.

Still reeling from the shock of the impact, she forced herself to a semi sitting position, supporting herself on her left elbow as the right one would not respond. Instinctively she began to check her body. Pain coursed through to her very soul. Her right arm and wrist resisted bending at all and the fingers of her left hand went off in different directions. There was a huge gash on her right thigh which was bleeding profusely, but as it was not spurting blood, she knew it was not an artery; a bone stuck through the skin just below the knee of her left leg. Both legs were bent in awkward positions and felt as useless as over cooked spaghetti.

"Definitely broken bones in both legs and arms", she thought.

Any attempt to raise her hips also resulted in intense pain and she felt at least one hip may have been broken as well. Taking a deep breath hurt; a sign of broken ribs? Tasting blood, he ran her tongue over her teeth and realized her two front teeth had been knocked out. Turning her head slowly to the right, she felt extreme nausea and could actually "track" the movement of her head. She could feel that it was warm and wet; all signs of a concussion ... Elizabeth knew she was in bad shape.

Experience told her that very few people hiked this section of the mountain and she was off the trail; as usual. Now, seriously injured and at least 10miles away from the nearest trail head (if she was even that close), her cell phone shattered in the fall, she was totally on her own.

"So, this is how it ends" she said out loud. "This is where I will die"

There would be no gentle passing into a brighter place. There would be no friendly tunnel of light with someone she loved waiting to guide her through. No sense of ecstatic freedom in her uncontrolled flight; just an abrupt, but painful and solitary termination of life.

Elizabeth, who had never feared death, now was bitterly disappointed in all that was to be lost to her. Making her way through a very ordinary but stress filled and difficult life, she knew that she would miss the desert and this mountain range. She would miss watching her puppy grow and seeing Jon's smile or hopefully hearing her sweet granddaughter's laughter once again. Family drama's, work, taxes and bills, government upheaval, loss of her breasts, and the continued spread of cancer were the hard parts of life, but oh there was so much beauty and joy in the world as well and right now all of the bad paled in comparison.

Tears flowed from her eyes, not because of pain as shock still shielded her from that, but more from something akin to homesickness which swept through her.

The only regret she now felt she had was in not seeing and doing as MUCH as she could in life and of leaving her poor puppy to fend for himself.

"I'm not ready yet God"' she thought and cried silent tears. "I have not lived"

She heard Ranger let out a painful yelp as he began to make his way down to her and she wanted to tell him to stay where he was... not to come to her. She was so afraid he would also fall and quite possibly to his death. However, when her beloved dog finally reached her, his brown almond eyes showed so much fear, love and concern, that she ended up reassuring him. "I'm okay boy. I'm okay"; she croaked, and was grateful for his warm presence.

He started to tug at her, trying to get her to walk, and when that did not work he began dragging her by the backpack still firmly strapped to her back. But she couldn't move and the pain caused her to scream.

Overhead, a red-tailed hawk, making tight circles in the sky, observed everything below. It screeched its piercing cry, twice, and continued to soar.

Seemingly in response to the hawk's cry, Ranger pulled back, tilted his head to one side and then the other as if considering his choices, nudged Elizabeth with his nose, gave her one gentle lick and then ran off, heading back up the trail barking all the way. Before long, the dog's cries for help were replaced by gusts of wind and Elizabeth began to feel the cold creep in; the exact opposite of the intense heat she had experienced throughout the day. She tried not to shake - the heat of the day had gone, and it was now cold and dark, but she was also so very afraid. She felt insects crawling over her. She had a morbid fear of spiders and scorpions and now could do nothing to avoid them. Then, suddenly, she felt the light patter of rain. The Monsoon had arrived. The patter rapidly became a torrent and the winds whipped the desert floor across her body like sandpaper as the ice cold enveloped her body.

Elizabeth started singing to herself; a version of "Brickyard Road" (written and performed by Johnny Van Zants) to fight off the blackness that threatened to engulf her;
"""" I know I can't bring back yesterday, but Lord won't you help me find my way. I want to go back, to Brickyard Road. God take me home, take me to Brickyard Road"""".

"An interlude of silence whispered through her ears like a ghost of flying arrowheads and coyotes

preying upon the labyrinth of dusty remains. Her ability to tread on, lifeless. Howling winds whipped passed her temples; the wolf on the inside trying not to move, just as her spirit passes through.

The deep ravine was pulling her forward, reaching the surface of the mountain in pursuit of this haunted terrain. A territorial asylum of the hunted, descending, where Indians in the Superstition wilderness surrendered, years ago – A Skeleton Canyon."

Was this really to be her grave?

At around 1 am, drenched, cold, broken and battered, with hyperthermia setting in, she was staring up at the mountain to the cave she had tried so desperately to reach, when she saw a bright light behind it.

She began to reach out for it - ready to give up - when a familiar voice said, "It's not your time yet, babe. There is so much for you to learn and do."

At that, she fell into blessed unconsciousness.

THE DREAM CATCHER OF LIFE

Humankind has not woven the web of life.
We are but one thread within it.
Whatever we do to the web, we do to ourselves.
All things are bound together
All things connect.

~Chief Seattle~

Memories, dreams…. or were they real. Elizabeth reached out for her pup but could not feel him anywhere. Opening her eyes, now acutely aware of the pain she was in, she squinted trying to see him. She tried whistling for him but missing teeth did not aid in that area. There was no answer from her beloved pet; no sign.

Trying to sit up brought excruciating pain which caused her to fall back and drift between waves of nausea and fighting off unconsciousness. She HAD to get to her feet. She had to find her companion… her fur baby. And she had to get off of this Mountain.

Peering through blurred vision, she saw a red tail hawk sitting on the distant ledge above her head. It appeared, to Elizabeth, that the hawk simply dissolved into the painting on the cliff face... so too did her consciousness dissolve again.

Once more, she roused herself and she looked up the Mountain path where the hawk had gone – now an Indian Maiden was standing on a boulder right in the exact same spot where she had seen the painting and she saw her beloved pet beside the maiden. Desperately she tried to hang on to consciousness – but it slipped away once again as she called out for him to come to her.

Ranger ran up to his beloved owner and sat beside her whining piteously tenderly licking her face; the wound on her head no longer bleeding.

The maiden motioned to someone further up the trail and four young Indian men moved quietly forward to join her. She ran over to Elizabeth and began to evaluate her injuries as her faithful companion continued to lick her face and paw at her shoulder which roused her to semi consciousness. Reaching out, she touched his paw, grateful for the physical contact, and then sank back into an oblivious darkness.

The men unrolled a travois, gently gathered Elizabeth onto it, removed the backpack that was still partially strapped to her back around her waist, and handed the pack to the woman, and as the darkness completely enfolded her they were taking her gently up the mountain trail. All that remained was the ever-watching hawk.

When Elizabeth came back to consciousness, it was pitch dark and she was thirsty; but she was still far too weak and in too much pain to make any effort to move. She was too weak and confused to even contemplate what had happened to her; it was as if she had been drugged.

She did not know where she was, but assumed she was still at the foot of the Mountain trail. At that moment, she did not care one way or another. Her only real concern was for her dog. Where was he? Was he close? Was he all right?

"Where are you boy?" she moaned. "I don't want to be alone out here without you... you are such a silly dog. You are too young to be alone. Where are you boy? Ranger?"

A cold nose and furry frame touched her cheek and lay down beside her. She suddenly felt a great peace and drifted back to sleep. This time it was sleep, and not a loss of consciousness. The next time she woke, it was morning but the sun had not yet risen. She could hear water running – it sounded wonderful! Before she could make any effort to move, an arm was slipped under her head and an earthen vessel of water was held to her mouth and a bitter sweet wetness passed through her lips.

"Where was she? Where was Ranger? Did Jon know she was missing yet?"

The fact is that when Jon had not received his customary instant messages, emails or face time with Elizabeth, he knew something was wrong. She had let him know that she would be heading to the Superstition Mountain and the general area in which she would be hiking. She and he always spoke, even when far away, every day, several times a day and always at 8:00 her time at night. He had contacted the park rangers at 10:00 p.m.

the night of the fall and search teams consisting of park rangers with search dogs, other volunteers, and helicopters now scoured the craggy slopes of the Superstition. Although they had found her jeep they had yet to find a single sign of her or her dog. The hours were ticking by and experience told everyone that the longer it took to find her, the less likely they would find her alive.

Jon boarded a plane for Mesa.

A TRUE WARRIOR

What is life?
"It is the flash of a firefly in the night
It is the breath of a buffalo in wintertime
It is the little shadow which runs across the grass
and loses itself in the sunset."
~Crowfoot~

She had initially met Jon over the
Internet, via an old website she had
established after her first book of poetry
was published. It was the poetry, and

more importantly the art work, that had led him to want to chat with the author. So an online relationship began that grew into one that had them meeting two years later and basically remaining together ever since. He would come down to Arizona in the late fall and stay with her until late spring; a relationship that allowed both the space to do the things life required of them; including providing some solitude.

One of the things that had initially attracted Elizabeth to Jon were his stories about his time in Viet Nam. Although he rarely talked about the trials of the war, he did often mention looking up through the dense overgrowth of the jungle and being able to see the stars... Even in all that ugliness he managed to find some peace and some beauty.

Jon was drafted into military service in May of 1969. For him—and lots of other men younger then him—there'd be no Summer of Love. In fact, the only music he danced to that summer was the maniacal cadence of his Drill Instructor, Staff Sergeant Hornet, as he marched his "worthless assholes" up and down two nasty bits of Fort Knox hill country known (un-affectionately) as Pain and No-Gain.

By November of 1969, he had graduated from Boot Camp and Medic training. He had also gone through some serious infantry/Ranger training. Although he thought himself a brave man, he never hesitated to tell anyone that the thought of running with Special Forces scared the shit out of him and kept him on his toes.

"After spending 20 hours on an airplane", Jon told Elizabeth; I will NEVER forget my first breath of "fresh" air as I stepped out the door and into the terrifying, sun-drenched brilliance of Vietnam. Laden with syrupy humidity, and reeking of urine and rotting vegetation, the stifling air clung to you like a damp shroud."

"However, it didn't take long for fear and adrenalin to override my sense of smell, and I was forced to quickly acclimate to the horrid odor and the oppressive humidity; I was already getting used to what was called "life" in Vietnam.

"As we filed off the airplane a sergeant pushed us into a misshapen formation and began marching us off the tarmac and to our initial round of in-country processing. Moving away from the aircraft we heard the sounds of laughter, shouting, and a rising tide of applause. With greenhorn eyes we watched in the silence of disbelief as a ragged, but cheerful, troop of soldiers walked past us heading in the opposite direction...."

"They greeted us with loud school-boy like laughter and profane comments, and reached out to shake our hands and pat us on the back."

"Good luck," one said to me as he grasped my hand. ""You're gonna need it,"" he called over his shoulder as he disappeared down the tarmac."

"It finally dawned on all of us that these guys were going home. They were getting on **our** plane and heading back home. **They were going back to our "World", safety, and sanity."**

Jon told Liz that is was like getting punched right in the gonads." I don't think any of us expected to see guys actually going home. It was so hard to take. We were looking at another 547 days, <u>minimum</u>, before we'd be heading back home; if, that is, we even managed to survive our full tour of duty. And, watching those guys as they headed for their 'freedom bird,' it now seemed like our eighteen months in Vietnam was never going to end."

Sadly, for many young Americans, that blessed homecoming never came.

Jon was told to report to the 57th Medical Company, at the Army Heliport, in Chu Lai. When he asked the sergeant what the 57th Medical Company was he said it was a medical evacuation outfit.

"They're "Dust Off", they fly helicopters," he added.

Having had a fear of heights since before he was born, Jon had been tempted to ask if it wasn't too late to sign up for the infantry as a simple ground pounder; they, at least, got to keep their feet on the ground. But, it was too late. By order of the great mysterious force that controlled all things military, Jon was headed for the city of Chu Lai, and the 57thth Dust Off.

As the fates would have it, Jon always said that he couldn't have asked for a better unit to serve in. He spent roughly 16 months and 21 days with the 57th and it was an experience and a time he would gratefully and sorrowfully never forget. So much so in fact, that Jon went over for three more tours when his first had ended... The ghosts haunted him always and Liz knew, from her own background in psychology, that he felt guilty for surviving.

The bravery, courage, and dedication to duty he saw exhibited everyday by the men who flew dangerous, life-saving missions—missions of mercy and hope—was simply incredible.

"Yes", thought Jon, "it was a privilege and an honor to have served with the men of the 57th Dust Off. I will forever hold them in awe and respect for the courage they displayed (in the most unassuming manner), the missions they accomplished, and the lives they saved."

Dust Off has its own acronym: Dedicated Unhesitating Service to Our Fighting

Forces. That pretty well describes Dust Off, and Jon was privileged to have witnessed that dedication and service first hand. As a medic (reassigned to that rate after the initial Special Forces group he had been assigned to was dismantled), Jon flew in those helicopters, sitting right behind the pilots seat on the floor, ready to jump down to save a life or remove a body. That special "seat" eventually cost him the hearing in his right ear.

The unit's dedicated unhesitating service to the fighting forces, combined with an excellent medical support system, contributed to the lowest mortality rate for the United States Armed Forces of any conflict in military history. The period of service in Vietnam also provided the 57th

Medical Detachment (RA) with its motto, "The Original Dust off," when all aeromedical evacuations became known by the 57th Medical Detachment's original radio call sign "Dust off."

When the 57th Medical Detachment (RA) was sent to Vietnam, it became the first unit to use the UH-1 helicopter for MEDEVAC in actual combat operations, evacuating more than 100,000 patients within the combat zone.

The heroes in the Dust Off saga were the pilots, crew chiefs, and medics who flew those rescue missions. If the skillful pilots in charge of the aircraft were the brains of the operation, then the crew chiefs were the backbone, and the medics the heart and soul. Jon NEVER felt himself any kind of hero... at times, in fact, he felt himself a failure.

"Courage," Winston Churchill said, "is the first of human qualities because it is the quality which guarantees all others." However, Jon felt that courage was what John Wayne once said... "Being scared to death and saddling up anyway".

The courage displayed by Dust Off crews, from Vietnam to the present day, underscores the character and the qualities of these selfless men—and now, women—who dare fly into harm's way to give aid and comfort to their fellow soldiers in time of need.

He had once told Elizabeth that "for a soldier there can be no finer calling."

"I wish I could share with you the all the acts of compassion and heroism that occurred while I was with the 57th Dust Off, but those are not my stories to tell. What I can tell you is that time and again I witnessed the pilots and crews of Dust Off flying off into the dangerous unknown on lifesaving missions. They braved monsoon storms (real monsoon storms that make those here in the desert seem like dew drops), enemy fire, and mechanical uncertainty in order to save lives; and it made no difference whether the person was a wounded American, a pregnant mama-san, or an enemy soldier.

"Today", Jon spoke hoarsely, "the word 'hero' has been devalued to the point of meaninglessness. Today you're a hero for helping your kid do his homework. But for me, when I think of what it takes to be a true hero, I picture four brave souls in a Huey helicopter flying off to some unknown jungle destination to rescue a wounded/dying soldier."

"I really don't have any friends", he had told Elizabeth when they first met, "and I'm pretty particular about who I want as a friend. The world is pretty much dog-eat- dog, and no one seems to care much for anyone else.; except for what they can get out of it. As far as I'm concerned, I'm really not a part of this messed up society. What I'd really like to do is have a home in the mountains, somewhere far away from everyone. Sometimes I get so angry with the way things are being run."

After hearing Jon's story and being able to see the soul of a man who came back from a horrible war but could still see the beauty of the stars and the sunset, how Elizabeth had wanted to find him a home near the Superstition in the desert... far away from the maddening crowd and the slow decay of the country that they both so loved. Like her, he was drawn to this mountain range; ever present and ever changing.

She had always told Jon that "she would give him the world if she could..."

She had said those same words to Hunter... over 40 years ago. She had tried and failed.

FORGOTTEN

"I seek strength, not to be greater than my brother
But to fight my greatest enemy – myself.
Make me always ready to come to you
With clean hands and straight eyes.
So when life fades, as the fading sunset,
My spirit may come to you without shame."
~Chief Yellow Lark~

Many veterans find it difficult to forget the lack of positive support they received from the American public during the Vietnam War. This was especially brought home to them on their return from the combat zone to the United States. Many were met by screaming crowds and the media calling them "depraved fiends" and "baby killers". Many personally confronted hostility from friends and family, as well as strangers. Some were spat upon.

After their return home, some veterans found that the only defense was to search for a safe place. These veterans found themselves crisscrossing the continent, always searching for that place where they might feel accepted.

Many veterans cling to the hope that they can move away from their problems. It is not unusual to interview a veteran who, either alone or with his family, has effectively isolated himself from others by repeatedly moving from one geographical location to another. The stress on his family is immense and sometimes he or she loses all contact with those families... Connecting with another is next to impossible.

In Elizabeth's first career as a counselor, she had also found that those veterans who suffer the most painful survival guilt are primarily those who served as corpsmen or medics; like her Hunter (who served in the Navy) and now Jon (who served in the Army). Many of these men were trained for a few months to render first aid on the actual field of battle. The services they individually performed were heroic. With a bare amount of medical knowledge and large amounts of courage, determination, and faith, they saved countless lives. However, many of the men they tried to save died or were dead before they could ever reach them. Many of these casualties were beyond all medical help, yet most corpsmen and medics suffer extremely painful memories to this day, blaming their "incompetence" for these deaths. Listening to these veterans describe their anguish and torment... seeing the heroin tracks up and down their arms or the bones that have been broken in numerous barroom fights is, in itself, a very painful experience.

Many were the nights, as Elizabeth lay beside a sleeping Jon, that she would hear him yell out and occasionally ramble about the things he had seen. How often she had heard him speak of what it was like to actually have to kill a man... or that no one really understood the ramifications of war unless they could "smell" it.

(Smiling inwardly now, Jon remembered how of often Liz would say how she "wanted to cut his nose off"; so acute had Nam made his sense of smell.) How well that became apparent to Liz was when they were out hiking in the Superstition

and the wind brought down a sickeningly sweet smell which literally turned Jon's stomach.

He looked at her and regretfully said, "I have to go back... I am sorry. "

As she had turned to follow him while he moved rapidly ahead of her, she noticed off to the side of the trail, the body of a coyote. A few feet away from her, on a higher rock stood its mate looking down. It was Elizabeth's first honest smell of "death"; but it was evidently and most certainly not Jon's first encounter with that sickeningly sweet odor.

In the same light, she saw his reflexive reaction whenever the Mesa helicopters flew overhead, which was often, in their search for a criminal on foot or a missing child. She understood that those were sounds that lived within his very soul.

Elizabeth understood, all too well, that the fantasy of living the life of a hermit plays a central role in many veterans' daydreams. Many admit to extended periods of isolation in the mountains, on the road, or just behind a closed door in the city. Some veterans have actually taken a weapon and attempted to live off the land. In truth this was the life she also dreamed of; meeting Jon had finally allowed her to start visualizing those dreams. Jon new Elizabeth wanted a "safe place" too.

"Damn it Liz! Where the hell are you?"
Jon thought as, exhaustedly, he nodded off
to sleep.

RECURRING NIGHTMARES

"Cannon fire lingers in my mind. I'm so glad that I'm still alive
And I've been gone for such a long time..."
~Jeff Christie

Flying into a combat operation near
Fire Support Base Veghel, Jon
stepped down from the bird to the
screams of wounded soldiers –

"Medic! Medic! Medic!"

Around him and others of the "Dust Off Team" were the deafening explosions of hand grenades, satchel charges, and rocket propelled grenade rounds – as well as rifle and machine gun fire.

With ground fire so heavy, their helicopter had no choice but to leave the area... leaving the ground team to fend for themselves on their own.

Jon, his team, the wounded, and the dying were pinned down. They were literally at the mercy of uncontrollable forces; the North Vietnamese Army were only about

10 feet away from him and two of his wounded charges.

A wave of cold washed through him, like a chilling shock. In a last ditch effort to survive, Jon thrust himself into an absolute denial of what was about to happen and threw himself across the bodies of his 2 wounded men. He knew pain and death were imminent...

Suddenly, he was awake and in an ice cold sweat. Instinctively he reached out his right hand for Elizabeth, only to remember that he was on the plane to Mesa and Liz was lost somewhere in the Superstitions.

Looking out the window, wiping cold sweat from his brow, he saw they were flying directly over the Superstition Range which meant they would be landing shortly.

Somewhere, deep within his mind, he heard a soft voice whisper... "Please -- find me...I am here. I am here..."

LEGEND BECOMES REALITY

"Life has no smooth road for any of us; and in the bracing atmosphere of a high aim the very roughness stimulates the climber to steadier steps, till the legend, "over steep ways to the stars," fulfills itself."

~William Doane~

Slowly regaining her senses and yet still in great pain, Elizabeth tried to discern where she currently was. Everything around her seemed surreal and out of place. She was surrounded by several men and women, beautiful men and women with long black hair, roman like noses, high cheek bones and dark eyes.

The men wore leather shirts and breechcloths. Their hair was long and did not seem to be tied back but held back from their faces by either bandanas or pieces of woven leather.

The women wore dresses made out of buckskin. Their long hair was either worn long and free or was tied into a bun and sometimes fastened with hair ornaments. Just like the men, the women wore shirts which were often decorated with beads or fringe. Moccasin shoes or boots with beads were the standard footwear worn by both sexes.

"I am among Indian's", Elizabeth said to herself. "Not Indians like Jimmy Dale and his friends-- but **real,** actual Indians of early days."

Looking around she noted that they were definitely in a cave of some kind and petroglyphs of old adorned the fire lit walls. In various areas small camp fires burned and women worked over them, cooking, grinding, cleaning...

In the distance, she saw a huge loom where a weaver worked tirelessly creating a blanket or rug in an intricate pattern. The colors reminded Liz of the

Painted Desert that she and Jon had driven across in a convertible the first time he took her to see the Petrified Forest. When she had literally walked through a forest of jewels.

Scattered about the floor of the cave were various pieces of pottery and rugs. Against the walls were spears, bows and arrows.

From the opening of the cave she heard the deep chanting of an Indian male... their chief or shaman she thought?

"Where the hell am I?" Elizabeth wondered.

Remembering the stories told to her by Jimmy Dale, Elizabeth then wondered if, perhaps, members of an Apache tribe, massacred near the Superstition were returning to and from the Spirit world through a Sipapu and that is where she now was?

"Oh boy", she thought, "Is your mind on some sort of wild journey now! You must have one hell of a brain injury. Before you know it you will be clicking your heels together and saying "" there is no place like home". You have to get a grip on yourself!" Pain engulfed her, a low moan escaped her lips, and she let her head fall back down to the support behind her.

Suddenly, a pretty Indian woman, with Ranger at her side, walked over to her, spoke something to her that Elizabeth could not understand, and made her drink some more of the bitter sweet liquid. The pain that had started to shoot through her body once again went away. Ranger lay down beside her and she felt his paw on her broken hand, the warmth of his body and his breath, as gently he licked her face. Smiling, she fell back into a much needed sleep.

THE SEARCH

The mountains, I become a part of it...
The herbs, the fir tree, I become a part of it.
The morning mists, the clouds the gathering waters;
I become a part of it.
The wilderness, the dew drops, the pollen...
I become a part of it.
~Navajo Chant~

There was so much time to think and pray during the three plus hour flight from Chicago to Mesa. On his previous flights to see Liz, just prior to landing, Jon was always able to look down upon the

Superstition Mountains. Most of the time that Mountain Range always seemed to welcome him home. Today, it appeared ominous and foreboding.

When Jon's plane touched down at Williams Gateway Airport in Mesa, Arizona, Jimmy Dale and a representative of the Pinal county Sheriff's Department were waiting to meet him. Having met Jimmy Dale a few times over the course of the past twelve years, Jon recognized him immediately as he passed through the arrival gate of the Williams Gateway Airport in Mesa AZ. Jon was always somewhat amazed at the appearance of this old half/breed; he seemed ageless to Jon.

Jimmy (who stood about 6'2) strode up to Jon on his long legs, took his carry-on bag from him, and gave him a big one-armed bear hug. He looked deeply into Jon's eyes and asked him if he were okay?

"I am fine Jimmy"; he responded stoically; he could never get used to Jimmy Dale's need to hug people or the way he seemed to be able to look right into the core of a person. "Thanks. Is there any news of Elizabeth yet?"

Shaking hands with the Deputy, while still speaking to Jimmy, Jon immediately asked him; "Have you found her?'

"Just her Jeep. Not a single sign of her, or that shepherd pup of hers yet", said

Jimmy. "They were inseparable you know."

The Deputy added; "The best members of our department's Search and Rescue are now combing the back side of the Superstition. The terrain is so jagged and treacherous that only elite members of the department's search and rescue units are allowed on the mountain top; searchers have had to rappel into crevices from helicopters to reach some of the areas we are searching."

"We understand that she preferred the more difficult and less tourist type trails. Is that true?"

"Very true"; said Jon. "She preferred hiking on more difficult and often solitary trails." Laughing gently to himself, he told Jimmy and the Deputy "she absolutely hated the fact that recreational hikers just could not seem to shut up and listen to the music and words of nature -- so she would try to get away from the beaten path to avoid them."

Shaking his head, sadly, he thought; "please don't let that very need for quiet and peace have been the very thing that destroyed her. She has survived so very much."

Authorities had been searching high and low for the 55-year-old who was known to be battling not only third stage breast cancer but also had epilepsy and a series of other health issues. Some of the members thought she was crazy for even hiking at all. They did not know the strong spirit of this woman or her need for what the Mountain brought. Perhaps no one, except Jon and Jimmy Dale, ever really did or would.

"Right now, Jon, we have about 150 searchers combing the mountains for her, utilizing dogs, horses, and a helicopter. We never set out to do a half-assed search" said the Deputy. "We will do everything possible to find her."

"Search-and-rescue teams assume that she probably fell and injured herself on one of the lesser walked trails"; Deputy

Chavez continued. "After all, we have been told that Elizabeth, despite her medical conditions, was a fairly experienced hiker."

"All of us searching, from the volunteers to the sheriff's department, called out to her on the first night and didn't get any type of response, so that area they considered to have been gone over with a fine tooth comb "; Jimmy Dale told Jon.

"Where was that, Jimmy?"

"About two miles from where she parked the Jeep. Up near Rogers Canyon; close to Hells Hole... one of the places she so wished to explore and I asked her not to do so alone. It is a cursed place among my people, Jon. Hell's Hole, near Tortilla Creek, was once known as the Skeleton Pit because of the numerous skeletons in the area from the slaughter of Native Americans - both Apache & Yavapai - by the United States Army throughout the 1864-68 campaigns. The body count records are agonizingly depressing when it comes to this campaign. It was something like 90 to 1. Ninety Apache and Yavapai killed to one Pima Scout or soldier wounded or killed. As I remember, only three soldiers were killed and five wounded during the entire event. My people, on the other hand were massacred; we believe their spirits will never rest.

Jon shuddered inwardly to think of her in that area of so much hatred and death; all alone. "Where the hell are you Liz?" he thought to himself

Breaking into his thoughts, Jon heard Jimmy Dale ask; "Shall we get you over to Elizabeth's house to let you drop off your things and rest up before heading back out to the mountain? Or, if you prefer, you can come and stay with me and the Mrs."

asked Jimmy. He wondered if Jon should be alone in that house without her right now.

"No, I want to go to the Superstitions right now! As of today, there are 151 people searching for Elizabeth. Maybe, if she hears **my** voice, she will answer. Just maybe..."

"Oh, and I want to go back to where the Jeep is and start from there Jimmy. Will you partner up with me?"

"Absolutely!"

Turning to the Deputy Sheriff, Jon said," as I have Elizabeth's Power of Attorney and a set of keys, may I take her Jeep back to her place with me or do you require it for any type of forensic work?" Jon felt he would need the jeep for transportation over the next several weeks; if he could not then he would have to also have to rent a car tonight.

"No, Mr. Nickels, you may take the Jeep with you. Forensics went over it with a fine tooth comb already. We know she did NOT go missing in or around the Jeep. If we need it for any reason, we will reach out to you."

LOVE FOUND NOW LOST?

Native American symbolism of the hummingbird is that it teaches us to go beyond time and to see that what happened in the past and what may happen in the future is not nearly as important as what is occurring now. It reminds us to hover in the moment, and to appreciate its sweetness. To drink deeply of the nectar of life.

Climbing into the Jeep, Jon caught the scent of Elizabeth's perfume; Rapture. She had purchased that perfume with him a few months after having to put her little blind Shih Tzu, Isis, to sleep at the age of 16. Until that day, she had worn nothing but Lavender spray so that Isis would always be able to recognize her by scent. How she loved that new perfume (but not as much as she missed her little dog).

Her love and tenderness with her two little dogs endeared her to him even more. *She always reached out to the "throw aways" and took them to her heart.*

"Reminds me of the old powder scents women of a by-gone era once wore"; he had told her when she first asked him if he liked how it smelled. "Yes, Liz... I like how it smells"; he now said out loud.

Jon reached forward and touched the ceramic humming bird that hung from the rear view mirror. He had given that to Elizabeth on their first trip to Tucson back in 2006 as she so loved to watch the humming birds that would come to her patio throughout the year seeking nectar. She had hung it there, that very day, and said she liked to watch it "flutter" around the jeep when she drove.

Memories were what would keep him going; for now. So he would go "home" and told Jimmy Dale that he appreciated his offer but he wanted to be closer to her. Despite his sometimes aloof demeanor, he deeply cherished the memories they had made together. He had never said "I love you" to her, but he did ask her once if she knew how much he cherished her? She never replied, but he noted the gentle smile that crossed her face and the softening glow in her eyes.

As it was now late afternoon and there was not much time for him to actually begin helping in the ongoing search, he touched base with a few more deputies and spoke to one of the dog handlers. There was not much news to be learned.

He made arrangements to meet with Jimmy Dale back at the townhouse at five the following morning, climbed back into the Jeep adjusting the seat to accommodate his longer legs, reset the rear view mirror to accommodate his height, and headed back towards Mesa

and the condo he had shared with her
since meeting her back in 2006

As he pulled into the complex he was
overcome with sadness. When they first
met, she had loved it here... he had too.
He always told her that she had found a
fantastic place to rent and had chosen the
best possible spot in the complex.

Together they had turned the patio into a
desert oasis. They had purchased
decorative lighting, and a chimnea. Then,
on their explorative hikes and travels
through Arizona , New Mexico, and Utah,
they had brought back cuttings of
different cacti and succulents which now
adorned the patio.

The wonderful evenings they had spent under a canopy of stars, candles aglow all around the patio and the chimnea blazing... They would talk of everything and nothing, listen to music from his or her I-Pad and just enjoy one another's company. Sometimes Liz would disappear inside and come out bearing two frosty glasses of vanilla ice cream and sarsaparilla, while other times she would bring out hot dogs and roast them over the open fire. Such wonderful, peaceful times.

In the early mornings, when she was not at work, they would sit on the patio enjoying coffee and watching the sunrise. The old pine tree next to the house literally glowed in the light and always felt like a protective friend to both of them.

Then Cancer struck her with a vengeance; first colon, then breast, then skin and later thyroid. The economy went upside down under Obama and she lost her well-paying position as an engineer.

Then the once well-kept community that had wonderful neighbors went to hell. Investors bought up properties all around her that had gone into foreclosure or short-sale and turned them into rentals; but they did not care what types of people they rented to. Slowly the area became a ghetto and her world unsafe and uncertain.

And then her adult children issued her an ultimatum; stop seeing him or not see her grandchildren or them... Jon watched her spirit slowly crumble as her strength and resolve said, "You have chosen, not me." She had not seen any of them since and he could tell the pain the emptiness that had caused; that he had caused.

"No! They caused!"; he said firmly to himself. "They never had to fucking see me, but that's not what they really wanted."

Opening the door to the townhome, he caught the smell of lavender; the scent she surrounded herself in to help with pain and stress. He felt the warmness of the house she had decorated, mostly for him, welcome him "home".

Heading up the stairs, he undressed, turned on the ceiling fan, laid down on the Queen-sized bed they had purchased together not more than 8 months ago, and flipped on the television.

The local news was on and it was discussing the search for Liz. The reports were not sounding promising.

Jon drifted off into a fitful sleep...

The next day, the search was focused on the higher regions of the Superstitions, where it's more likely someone would fall or hurt themselves. Jon, having heard of a civilian Search and Rescue through conversations with Liz, called the Superstition Mountain Search and Rescue Team, and learning they had considerable more success in finding lost hikers in the area, requested they join the search.

After 10 more days of combing the landscape, Jon could tell that the Sherriff's Department and the SSRT were ready to end the search. Not one sign of Elizabeth or the dog could be found in a month of non-stop professional search.

It was as if the Mountain had somehow just swallowed them up.

A DOG NAMED NO

To the Native American a Dog is the guardian of loyalty and symbolizes guidance, loyaty and trust. Seeing a dog Animal Spirit in your dream, indicates a skill that you have ignored or forgotten, but needs to be activated. Your own values and intentions will enable you to go forward in the world and succeed.

When she woke, feeling much more rested and in a great deal less pain, she watched as the Apache families went about their daily tasks. She called to

Ranger who was out playing with a spotted Indian dog and he stopped long enough to send out a bark and a tail wag her way, but went on playing.

Taking in everything around her, Elizabeth realized she was captivated by Lolotea who was apparently her appointed care taker and whom also apparently had her Ranger. One day as Lolotea sat next to her, she became so overcome with her grace and serenity that she reached out to touch her. She grasped her arm and the Weaver, whom Elizabeth had learned was called Nana, stood up; she also caught a movement from the Shaman, Noch-Del-Klinne. A wave of fear washed over her; she instinctively knew that her action would not be tolerated; that she must treat this Lolotea with careful consideration.

She released her grasp and sank back down on her pallet feeling alone and destitute. Ranger, sensing her fear and pain, came running over and laid across her chest as if to say; "it's okay, I am here and I will protect you."

"I love you, boy", she said as she snuggled her face into his fur and let her tears fall. How often, while they were in the real world, had she turned to her loving fur boy for comfort and resolve? He had always been there.

Calmed by his presence, Elizabeth fell asleep.

The following day, Lolotea appeared and sat by Elizabeth again. This time Elizabeth burst out: "I just wish you could talk to me!"

"But, I can talk to you," she responded softly; taking Elizabeth by surprise.

"Well, why haven't you, then?" And as she was struck with a new thought, added: "And in my language, too!"

Lolotea laughed, a familiar tinkling brook-water sound, and answered: "You did not ask me before. And we are not actually talking in ANY language, just from one mind to another. In order to truly communicate, one must open their mind to another's to talk to him."

Suddenly a thought came to Liz that she had heard this "voice" before.

Liz had so many questions but the most important at the moment, was about Ranger. Elizabeth begged her to tell her how to approach her beloved puppy so that he would stay at her side and not leave her; like he used to before the terrible fall. Since the accident, Ranger, although checking in on Elizabeth when he sensed her pain or that she was troubled, seemed distant and almost reproachful of her now, and Liz could not understand why.

Lolotea responded "first must come true desire and faith – nothing is ever possible without desire and faith. When one desires deeply enough – believes deeply enough, she can open her mind to another (be it human, spirit, or animal,) and if that other wanted to communicate, both minds are open and tuned to each other."

"But understand this", your dog "No", feels you are badly hurt because of him. "No's spirit has been shattered. He fears for your life and loves you, but feels he is a bad dog. "No" travels with me for reassurance and love but comes to you at night to give you that same reassurance and love that you have always needed from him."

"No?" Elizabeth repeated. "No?" Oh dear God, Lolotea... his name is not "No" Where did you get that idea?

"From him", replied Lolotea; pointing at Ranger

Elizabeth was not entirely convinced. She pointed to her pup, now almost fully grown, growling, barking, and playing with the other Apache dogs. "My _dog_ told you his name was NO?"

Again, through her lilt of amusement Lolotea said, "They are not actually talking as such, although we do have words and our chants are words. But mostly they are just making sounds somewhat like the singing of birds.

However, if you listen, they do speak to us"

Elizabeth stopped to listen for a moment and realized she was right... the dog's noisy "speech" between one another, actually did sound like words."

"Lolotea, his name is not No. His name is Ranger. *(Funny, she thought, I always wondered what he thought his name was).* You see, I say no to him a great deal because he is such a mischievous boy and I try to teach him right from wrong to keep him safe. I always felt that maybe he thought his name might be No, or Get Down, or Stop That; but it's Ranger. He has a regal name, in my opinion. Since you appear capable of actually talking to him, please, let him know that for me. Let him know he is MY Ranger Danger..."

"In time, my friend, perhaps he will learn this and trust himself again, in the same way you must learn to do the same. Both of your spirits are seeking solace. For now, it is time for you to rest."

THE HEALING CEREMONY

"Seek the wonder of
Life and love,
For it lasts but a short time.
Open your heart to the unknown,
Though it may bring fear or pain
Believe that the Creator
Will guide you,
For there are grand rewards
Within Mystery"
~Blackhawk~

The days slipped by into what Elizabeth thought must be weeks, and finally she could manage to sit up and hobble about with assistance. One morning, Lolotea and another woman came to her and said that their shaman had decided to perform a healing ritual for her. She would be prepared that evening.

From her pallet, Elizabeth watched as the ground was cleared at the back of the cave between the fire and the western wall, over a space about six feet in diameter, and covered with a layer of clean sand. Here, Noch-Del-Klinne, their Shaman, bent down and began painting. The sand painting that first day contained the figures of snakes only, having their heads directed toward the west, with the exception of the sun symbol, which was drawn each day during the ceremony around a shallow hole, six or eight inches in diameter, at the center of the painting.

The sun was represented by a ring of white sand around the margin of the hole; next came a circle of black, and then a ring of red with white rays. After the painting had been completed, the shaman, dressed in white beaded leather, prepared for the occasion, and passed into the cave, on the floor of which four coyote tracks had been made leading to the dry painting.

Helping Elizabeth to her feet, Lolotea and Dahteste brought her over to the painting, having her step upon the footprints leading to the sand painting on which the shaman had spread kut-u-tin (cattail pollen) and sacred corn meal. She was then made to lay down upon the painting, facing the east. Songs were sung and prayers were offered to the sun, after which the women brought food from the camps into the special enclosure of the cave. Those who were within this section of the cave seated themselves around the wall and were served by the doorkeeper, who began at the left and carried food to each in turn. After all were served, the doorkeeper gathered a morsel of food form each and threw it outside of the caves enclosure, as a sacrifice to the sun, followed by prayers. Then the door keeper returned to the sacred area of the cave and ate his meal, as did Elizabeth. The remaining food was gathered for the next meal. The men carried the food vessels from the area into another section of the cave for the women to remove later.

Elizabeth was helped back to her pallet and as darkness fell, she watched as the men again painted snakes on the floor of the cave where the sacred fire had been built. A young pine tree was placed at the right and another at the left of the sand painting. All children were kept away from this area.

The next morning, they brought Elizabeth back and had her offer pollen and meal before she seated herself upon the painting. Suddenly, a terrifying figure rushed into the semidarkness of the lodge, lunged toward her, but seemed unable to reach her, gave forth two to three cries similar to a coyote pup and then made his exit.

Although she knew that it was only one of the men in disguise, Elizabeth still had been frightened. Hell that was an understatement... she was scared to death and her head still "tracked" whenever she moved it.

While the coyote figure was in the lodge, the singing men yelled at the tops of their voices to scare the coyote away. Elizabeth fell shaking to the ground. An eagle feather was waved rapidly to and fro above her head as she continued to seize and cry out. She thought, for sure, she was dying. Noch-Del-Klinne placed a live coal in a dish of blue corn meal and allowed her to inhale the smoke which quieted her somewhat as she sat upright, staring like one who was catatonic. Noch-Del-Klinne then handed her the medicine pipe filled with a special tobacco. After smoking this, Elizabeth recovered her senses and the pain in her head finally eased.

Two or three songs concluded this day's serious part of the ceremony. Elizabeth, now considered on the mend, was moved to the north side of the cave and remained there for the rest of the evening. A coyote rug was spread over the sand painting, and the sacred basket given to Noch-del-Klinne was inverted with the hide over the hole in the center of the painted area. The rug was then doubled over the basked and the margin of the hide was held down by the feet of the men sitting around. The white basket was ornamented with conventional red butterflies.

Noch-Del-Klinne began beating on the basket as if it were drum, striking it four times as a signal for the whole tribe to gather inside for the dance. Two notched sticks were placed upon the basket, a black one on the east side and a white one on the west side. The sticks were laid with one end resting upon the drum and the other end upon the ground. A tarsal bone of a deer was rubbed across the notches, at the sound of which the young women began to dance.

The women occupied the southern portion of the enclosure and the men arranged themselves along the opposite wall. The cave was brilliantly lighted by a circle of fires around the inside wall. The women's dance was ended by repetition of the same drum signal by which it had begun – four stokes upon the basket drum.

When the drum again sounded, those afflicted with ailments of any kind placed their hands upon the affected part of their bodies and made a hand gesture of casting off the disease. When the sticks were scraped again, the women chose partners from the men and boys and all danced together. This became the lighter aspect of the ceremonies: serious thoughts, the desire to please the gods, and the awe inspired by the Shaman and the deity represented in the coyote. This all gave way to a light-hearted merrymaking spirit, which by no means exhausted itself before the sound of the drum ceased, about midnight. Then, the voice of one of the elders was heard; telling all within the sacred circle to disperse to their own resting places.

The second day's ceremony resembled that of the first except the figures outlined in the sand were of bears, coyotes, bobcats and other animals, with here and there a snake. Elizabeth was not induced into a trance, nor was the general ceremony of casting off of disease performed.

The third day differed only in the character of the sand painting. Animals differed from those of the previous day and the elk and the horse seemed to dominate them.

On the fourth day, the figures of two deities were drawn in the dry painting, along with all kinds of animals. A black circle outside the painting symbolized the river. The program of the evening consisted of two groups of men, painted and dressed in the manner prescribed by the tradition of their ancestors

One party of the six men were the clowns with bodies and limbs painted with white and black horizontal rings. Ragged remnants of old blankets served as loincloths. On necks and shoulders appeared necklaces and festoons of bread, which had been baked in small fantastic shapes. Four wore old buffalo skin caps, with the skin sewed to look like buffalo horns, projecting laterally and downward; to one horn was attached an eagle feather, to the other a turkey feather. Two men dressed their hair in the shape of horns.

The other group of twelve men, painted white with oblique black stripes extending downward from the inner corners of their eyes, wore necklaces and an eagle feather in their hair. Bands of pine brush were wrapped around their waists, arms, and ankles.

As on the other evenings, the women began the dance; then the general dance followed in which the women selected their partners from among the men. Then the two deities entered the cave and marched directly to the medicine circle around which four circuits were made in a sun wise direction. The twelve then took positions on the south side of the pathway from the gate to the lodge. Clowns ran about among the crowd. Two men led the singing and also took the lead during the exit back through the medicine circle. The dance continued until sunrise.

As the sun rose above the mountain, every man, woman, and child joined in the dance. Elizabeth looked on in awe and joy with Ranger sitting beside her, often resting his head on her lap or licking her face or hand as she tenderly pet him. The ceremony again took on a serious nature, as the sun's rays clear and bright in that rare and arid atmosphere, lit up the valley and the whole band of Apaches marched in line out of the cave toward the sun.

Noch-Del-Klinne led the way, carrying the two young pines from the end of the dry sand painting, along with the scared basket containing the meal. Each person marched past Elizabeth and took a pinch of the meal from the basket and cast it upon the pine trees. The line was reformed, facing the lodge, then one of the older men stepped forward and shook his blanket four times. At this signal, all shook their blankets to frighten away diseases and then ran back inside the cave.

The ceremonies ended. Lolotea came up beside Elizabeth and offered her a bowl of cool water, called to Ranger who jumped up to follow her, and left her alone to sleep and wonder...

THE WEAVER

"You see, when weaving a blanket, an Indian woman leaves a flaw to let the soul out."

One afternoon after Lolotea and Ranger had left her alone to travel the outside world, Elizabeth got up, hobbled over to the Weaver, and sat down near her. If desire was the key, she had plenty of that! She desperately wanted to find out what was going on. No, she NEEDED to understand so that, maybe, she could get back to her normal life.

It required several days and endless attempts at communicating and listening to the thoughts of various members of the tribe as they went about their daily lives, but finally she learned more about the people she was now with. This was an ancient tribe that had been set up to come out through the Sipapu and inhabit the Earth once again, just as she had imagined in a dream state so long ago.

"This is too incredible!" she thought to herself. "Maybe what I thought was a dream several years ago was actually them?" Then she remembered trying to find where a tinkling fairy like sound was coming from on many of her hikes... the same sound she now heard whenever Lolotea spoke to her.

Elizabeth learned that this was a period of time that the Apache referred to as a "linking year"; when they were working towards gathering all those things needed to help them settle a new area on earth. Previous members of their tribe had built many such dwellings and several villages throughout the Southwest. She learned, also, that Lolotea was the beloved daughter of Usen, the Supreme Spirit, and only because of that could she be in the world, as a human; for just this season.

Elizabeth asked the Weaver "will Lolotea be allowed to come out with the new settlers of the world?"

Nana assured her that she would not; her father would probably never let her leave the Spirit World again as he cherished his daughter greatly and knew the evil of the earth. "The Great Spirit wishes to help heal the earth, which is why he sought to return the Apache, but would not risk his only daughter", she told Elizabeth.

But, will she let my dog stay here now? With me? Or will they both disappear for good when the season ends?

Elizabeth was met with silence as the Weaver had closed her mind and communication had stopped. For now, Elizabeth had to be content with the small amount she had learned and try to formulate a plan from there.

Elizabeth was certainly not content with the prospects of losing her beloved dog; her fur-child and her closest friend. Since her daughter had ripped her granddaughter away from her, she had felt tremendously alone. Ranger had taken all that away from her and given her love and peace in return. If Lolotea returned to her plane and took him with her, then Elizabeth needed to figure out how she was going to go through the Sipapu to be with him and maybe, one day, come back through together.

"I won't lose anything else I love"; she said firmly. "I will die first!!"

It took another day or two for her to get the Weaver to talk to her again. She seemed to be afraid to say very much, but at last Elizabeth asked her point blank if there was ANY way she could go back through the Sipapu with them. The Weaver was stark silent for a moment and Elizabeth thought she had angered her.

"Damn, she thought, why had she been so blunt?" Apparently the Weaver heard her.

"With Faith, anything is possible," the Weaver hoarsely whispered.

"ANYTHING is possible?" "Anything is possible." Elizabeth repeated this idea over and over again in her mind.

"But only with faith."

The Weaver paused in her work to give Elizabeth her undivided attention; something she had not done before, and Elizabeth was almost sorry now that she had because of the severe look on her face.

"Only with faith!!! You! Talk to Shaman!"

That said, the Weaver's mind snapped shut, ending the discussion, and Elizabeth had to return to her pallet to think this over.

GUIDANCE

"When you are in doubt, be still and wait'
When doubt no longer exists for you, then go forward with
courage.
So long as mists envelop you, be still;
Be still until the sunlight pours through and dispels the mists
As surely it will.
Then act with courage"
Native American~unknown~

Needless to say, Elizabeth was in total
awe of the Shaman. She understood and

respected how the Indians revered these leaders. She knew, almost instinctively, that she just could not simply walk up to him and start asking a bunch of questions. If she could just take some gift—her mind searched for something. She had not had need for any of the clothing or her backpack which the Indians had removed when she was first brought here, but looking around for them now, she spotted the clothes cleanly washed and folded on a little shelf along the far wall and hanging from a large peg, right beside it, was her backpack. She hobbled over to them, supporting herself on the intricately carved and turquoise laden walking stick Lolotea had provided her with, and inventoried the contents of her back pack. She decided upon the bowie knife her birth father, George, had given to her almost 20 years ago, and carried it back to her pallet where she again rested and gained strength.

When she finally worked up the courage, she approached the Shaman and knelt down as she had watched the young children that the Shaman often taught do. The old seer looked up, smiled, and opened his mind to Elizabeth, as she said "I have a gift for you wise one."

She took the knife out of the sheath and pulled a hair form her head and snipped it off an inch or so from where she held it in her fingers. She was glad she always kept the edge honed razor sharp as Jon had taught her and the blade gleamed in the sunlight.

Noch-del-Klinne, looked at the knife in her outstretched hand, then reached behind himself, struck off a chip of flint, and, taking a hair from his own head he indicated that Elizabeth should hold one end. Then he delicately and carefully split the hair with the flint. She watched the little curls of spider-web fineness curl up and suddenly she understood – they did not need ANY of her so-called technology. Their culture was not physical, it was so much more refined than the world of today and their stone tools were certainly more than adequate. The Apache no longer had to make war... The meeting was congenial, however, and Elizabeth offered the knife anyway. Noch-del-Klinne smiled, nodded his acceptance, and thanked her for the gift with a gracious poise worthy of royalty.

Deep within, Elizabeth realized that her own perception had been considerably sharpened by this experience.

After a short time had passed, she looked at the old wise one again. She had to know and was certain this was the only way she could find out. As carefully as she could, she asked if it would be possible for a mortal to go back through a Sipapu, saying that although she knew Lolotea loved her dog with all of her heart, so did she and if her dog was to be taken into the other world, the only true friend and family she had left, then Elizabeth wanted to go as well and be with him and the tribe for all time and eternity.

Noch-de-Klinne chipped silently at the magnificent arrowhead for what felt like a very long span of time and Elizabeth was beginning to fear that he would not answer her. Eventually, the old man held out the arrowhead for her to inspect. Then he took it back, laid it carefully on a second flint, and with one chip broke it into two pieces.

Smiling wisely, he said "There are ways to do everything if one has the desire and the patience to learn."

He handed the two pieces of flint to Elizabeth to make his point.

After another lengthy period of silence, the Shaman said that this matter had already come up in the Council.

"The council is aware of Lolotea's great attachment to Ranger and would not be able to deny her the right to take the dog back with her to the spirit world; if that is what she AND the dog desired. They are also aware, however, of Elizabeth's great love and need for the dog - as well as the dog's love and need for her. Therefore, it depended on the dog and Elizabeth. If she wanted to learn the rituals and chants and then go through the spiritual teachings for purification then, and only then would she, perhaps, be able to go through the Sipapu and maybe return to her own time."

Noch-Del-Klinne said, "Should you wish to properly prepare yourself, you may begin learning tomorrow." We feel you are mended enough in body to do so; it is your spirit that now needs healing."

Elizabeth's heart sang and she hobbled to the doorway, she let out a bellowing yawp to the red tail hawk circling above... and the hawk answered.

A good omen!!

The Making of an Apache Warrior...

"When you were born, you cried
And the world rejoiced.
Live your life
So that when you die,
The world cries and you rejoice" ~White Elk~

As Elizabeth's preparations continued for her eventual entry into the spiritual realm of the Apache through the Sipapu, she was often invited to participate in, or at least attend and witness, some of the ancient ceremonies that would prepare the youth of the tribe for manhood/womanhood. Through these ceremonial rites of passage, Elizabeth somehow also learned more about the pains within her own life and that of her Hunter and her Jon. One such time came as a young male was being made ready to become a warrior...

Noch-Del-Klinne explained to Elizabeth that in preparation to become a warrior an Apache youth must have gone with the warriors of his tribe four separate times on the warpath. In this instance, as time was innocuous in the realm of the Sipapu, this had occurred for a young male called Tarak (which means Star in Apache) who had performed this feat over what would have been several decades in the outside world.

"On the first trip he was given only very inferior food. With this he had to be contented without uttering a single complaint. On none of the four trips was he ever allowed to select his food as the warriors do, but had to eat the food he was permitted to have."

"On each of these expeditions he was to act as a servant; caring for the horses, cooking the food, and doing whatever duties he should do without being told. He knows what things are to be done, and without waiting to be told to do them. He is not allowed to speak to any warrior except in answer to questions or when told to speak."

"During these four wars he is expected to learn the sacred names of everything used in war, for after the tribe enters upon the warpath no common names are used in referring to anything appertaining to war in any way. War is a solemn religious matter."

"If, after four expeditions, all the warriors are satisfied that the youth has been industrious, has not spoken out of order, has been discreet in all things, has shown courage in battle, has borne all hardships uncomplainingly, and has exhibited no color of cowardice, or weakness of any kind, he may by vote of the council be admitted as a warrior. However, if any warrior objects to him for any reason he will be subjected to further tests, and if he meets these courageously, his name may again be proposed. When he has proven beyond question that he can bear hardships without complaint, and that he is a stranger to fear, he is admitted to the council of the warriors in the lowest rank. After this there is no formal test for promotions, but by common consent he assumes a station on the battlefield, and if that position is maintained with honor, he is allowed to keep it, and may be asked, or may volunteer, to take a higher station, but no warrior would presume to take a higher station unless he had assurance from the leaders of the tribe that his conduct in the first position was worthy of commendation."

Tarak had passed each test with apparent ease and the first vote of the council gave him warrior status. How proud he was.

Elizabeth was surprised to learn that, other than the election of the tribe's chief, this was the ONLY election held by the council in formal assembly.

She also learned, through Noch–del–Klinne, that old men are not allowed to lead in battle, but their advice is always respected and sought out.

"Old age", he told her, "means loss of physical power and is fatal to active leadership".

This was very similar, she thought, as to how the modern-day military was run. The older more seasoned men were the trainers and planners while the younger men, sadly, were on the front lines; where once her Hunter and Jon had also been. One, Hunter, a warrior of the sea and the other, Jon, a warrior of the land; both trained healers in a time of so much anger, hate, and destruction. Hunter near the end of the Vietnam War and during the Israeli Conflict in the Baltic Sea, and Jon, during the worst of the Vietnam War from 1968 thru 1974.

SUNRISE CEREMONY

In the early 1900s, when the U.S. government banned Native American spiritual practices and rituals, conducting the Sunrise Ceremony was an illegal act; as a result, its practice diminished, and those ceremonies that did occur were conducted secretly...

Through the teachings of Lolotea and Nana, Elizabeth learned that the first woman, White Painted Woman (also known as Esdzanadehe, and Changing Woman) survived the "Great Flood in an abalone shell, and then wandered the land as the waters receded. (Elizabeth was amazed that, just as in her Catholic upbringing, the Apache also had a Great Flood that destroyed the evil that was then upon the land.) Atop a high mountain, Esdzanadehe was impregnated by the sun, and gave birth to a son; Killer of Enemies (Apache). Soon afterwards, she was impregnated by the Rain, and gave birth to Son of Water.

However, the world the people lived in was not safe until White Painted Woman's sons killed the Owl Man Giant who had been terrorizing the tribe.

(Big Owl also plays a more important mythological role as an early adversary of the War Twins. Like other legendary Apache beings, Big Owl is sometimes described as having human form (in this case a man-eating ogre) and other times *animal form (in this case a horned owl*

large enough to carry off a child.)

When they returned from their victory, bringing the meat they had hunted, White Painted Woman expressed a cry of triumph and delight, which later will be echoed by the godmother of the young girl at the Sunrise Ceremony. She was then guided by Usen to establish a puberty rite to be given for all daughters born to her people, and to instruct the women of the tribe in the ritual, and the rites of womanhood.

When she became old, White Painted Woman walked east toward the sun until she met her younger self, merged with it, and became young again. Thus repeatedly, she is born again and again, from generation to generation.

Traditionally all Apache girls were required to complete the sunrise ceremony, also known as Na'ii'ees or the puberty ceremony, during the summer following their first menstruation. The four-day ceremony is a ritual reenactment of the Apache Origin Myth and through personification draws the female participant closer to the first woman, White Painted Woman.

The Sunrise Ceremony serves many purposes - personally, spiritually and communally - and is often one of the most memorable and significant experiences of Apache females in today's world, just as it was for Apache women in the past.

First, by re-enacting the Creation myth, and personifying White Painted Woman, the girl connects deeply to her spiritual heritage, which she experiences, often for the first time, as the core of herself. In her connection to White Painted Woman, she gains command over her weaknesses and the dark forces of her nature, and knows her own spiritual power, sacredness and her goodness. She also may discover her own ability to heal.

Second, she learns about what it means to become a woman, first through attunement to the physical manifestations of womanhood such as menstruation (and learning about sexuality), as well as the development of physical strength and endurance. The rigorous physical training she must go through in order to survive four days of dancing and running is considerable, and surviving and triumphing during the "sacred ordeal" strengthens her both physically and emotionally.

Lolotea told Elizabeth; "most Apache women who have experienced the Sunrise Ceremony say afterwards that it significantly increased their self-esteem and confidence. When it ended, they no longer felt themselves to be a child; they truly experienced themselves as "becoming a woman."

Third, the Apache girl entering womanhood experiences the interpersonal and communal manifestations of womanhood in her culture - the necessity to work hard, to meet the needs and demands of others, to exercise her power for others' benefit, and to present herself to the world, even when suffering or exhausted, with dignity and a pleasant disposition. Her temperament during the ceremony is believed to be the primary indicator of her temperament throughout her future life.

Not only does she give to the community - food, gifts, healings, blessings, but she also joyfully receives from the community blessings, acceptance and love. Throughout the ceremony, she receives prayers and heartfelt wishes for prosperity, wellbeing, fruitfulness, a long life, and a healthy old age.

Finally, the Sunrise ceremony serves the community as well as the girls entering womanhood. It brings extended families and tribes together, strengthening clan obligations, reciprocity and emotional bonds, and deepening the Apache's connection to his or her own spiritual heritage.

"Today and for the next four days", said Lolotea, "you will be present as one of our young women begins her passage into woman hood. It is a difficult ceremony but beautiful in its meaning and method."

Elizabeth was humbled, honored, and very excited to be allowed to attend this ceremony; even more so than she had been to sit on the outside of the passage of a boy into manhood.

"Of course that would make sense", she thought to herself... "I am a woman". At that she smiled to herself and felt a tear roll down her cheek.

Most, if not all, of the extended family of an Apache girl are involved in preparing her puberty ceremony. The most central figure is the sponsoring godmother, followed by the Shaman and Gans Crown Dancers.

"The family takes special care in choosing the godmother, who will be a role model and have a special relationship with the girl throughout her life."

"As her primary attendant in the Sunrise ceremony, the godmother will dance with her both day and night, massage her, help inspire her and care for her when she is exhausted, give her food and drink, and prepare a huge dinner for all her relations. She therefore must be strong, energetic and very committed. "

Elizabeth smiled when she heard this as she remembered her own godmother, Lucy, and the wonderful relationship she had with her growing up...

"Oh how I love and miss you Lucy", she whispered.

Lucy had not been young when she became Elizabeth's Godmother; she was around 54 and Liz just 4 and a half years old when the baptismal occurred. Lucy stood only 4'8", if she were even that tall, but oh she had so much energy and strength and wisdom.

She could dry Liz's tears in an instance, make her feel safe, and cook the greatest Italian food ever created...

When Elizabeth had been 16 years old, she was left at home on Halloween to attend to the costumed Halloween celebrants. Hunter was already in the Navy and out to sea and Liz, already in college, never went out on Halloween. That night, she opened the door to a small trick or treater in a gorgeous clown outfit and a full mask. As she went to place candy into the child's bag, the child forced its way into her parent's dining room.

Liz, not wanting to lose her temper with a child, turned around and firmly but politely said that she could NOT be inside the house and would need to leave immediately.

At this, the child placed its candy bag on the dining room table and proceeded to turn summersaults around the table. When it stood up... the child removed its mask to reveal.... LUCY! ... who was then in her mid - late 60s. Oh yes, Lucy would have definitely fit the requirements of an Apache Godmother. Yes indeed!

"Everyone should have a wonderful grandmother like that" Liz told Lolotea who had been listening to her thoughts, as another tear rolled down her cheek.

"When choosing a godmother", Lolotea continued, "the family visits her residence at dawn, and places an eagle feather on her foot, offering her also a prayer stone and gifts as they request her to serve as godmother to their daughter. They may only ask four godmothers; acceptance is indicated by picking up the feather from her foot."

The Shaman also has an important role, and must be approached in a similar manner. The Shaman will prepare the sacred items used in the four-day event, including an eagle feather for the girl's hair, deer skin clothing, and paint made from corn and clay.

He will preside over much of the ceremony, chanting dozens of songs and prayers, and both orchestrating and paying the singers and drummers that will accompany him; the Gans (Mountain Spirit) Crown Dancers. The dance itself lasts three to six hours and is performed twice to 32 songs and prayers. The Crown Dance or Mountain Spirit Dance is a masked dance in which the participants impersonate deities of the mountains—specifically the Gans, or mountain spirits.

"That kind of sounds like my Godfather", Liz excitedly told her. Oh he did EVERYTHING for special occasions for me... my Uncle Bill.

How very true that was and in more ways than the outside world once knew. He taught her how to make a Thanksgiving dinner when she was 14. He colored Easter eggs with her EVERY year of her childhood. He decorated Christmas cookies. He watched movies with her late at night; old film noir black and white ones which she

loved so much. More importantly, he
LISTENED to her and he taught her to love
books and classical music and museums.
He even taught her to hem pants and
skirts.

He kept her safe from pain; at least on the
weekend he was at her parent's home. He
kept her safe...

What he did not do for her though was ever
accept Hunter. Ever!

Lolotea paused while Elizabeth's thoughts
spoke loudly to her and then continued:
"Another female relative, usually an older
sister or cousin, is also actively involved,
dancing along with the girl throughout
much of her ceremony, supporting her
when her energy flags."

As this information was imparted, a great sadness suddenly grabbed at Elizabeth's heart – envy crossed her mind momentarily as she would have liked to of had an older sister or cousin who could have helped support her through life. That dream never did some true; the family she had so longed for never came true... Several tears overwhelmed the banks of her eyes and slid down her cheek. Lolotea sensed the black hole within her soul.

Ranger was suddenly at Elizabeth's side, sensing her sorrow, as Lolotea sadly smiled at both and walked off to speak with Noch-Del-Klinne

Elizabeth was already aware that the Sunrise Ceremony involved extensive preparation and teaching, often lasting six months or more before the ritual actually could begin. Much of the preparation, such as creating the girl's highly symbolic costume, and building the lodge, required following complex procedures and rituals; another facet of preparation was an exercise regime oriented toward strengthening the girl's physical endurance. Her family was also engaged in extensive food preparation, since throughout the ceremony, they would be providing food and gifts to all participants and visitors.

Once the actual ceremony began, the young girl was guided by her sponsor and the Shaman through its many stages, including hours each day and night of dancing (the number of hours increasing each day and night), often in tandem with a female cousin whom she had chosen as a means of support through the ceremony. She was also required to run; and I mean RUN! These rituals of running were very important - running east toward the sun at dawn, and running toward all four directions - symbolically through the "four stages of life." Elizabeth could not help but worry about the exhausting pace the young girl was forced to maintain, the limited amounts of food and sleep she could have and marveled at her strength and fortitude.

Elizabeth watched as the young girl, Sonsee-aray, which Liz learned meant "Morning Star takes away Clouds", reenacted Changing Woman's story. She watched as her sponsor (godmother), Ishton, massaged the girl's body so that she was "molded" into Changing Woman. There was endless singing, chanting and praying throughout most of the night. There were nightly dances of the Ga'an or Mountain Spirits and the accompanying clown, and the throwing of buckskin blankets toward the four directions.

The young girl was also covered with a sacred mixture of cornmeal and clay, which she could not wash off throughout the entire ceremony. During the last day, she blessed her people with pollen, as well as "healed" all members of her tribe who sought her healing touch and blessing.

Surprisingly, Sonsee-aray came over to Liz and sprinkled pollen on her as well.

She also received many gifts from her people celebrating her entry into womanhood.

While watching all of this come to pass, vivid visions and dreams came into Elizabeth's waking and sleeping moments.

> ➤ She remembered her first communion and the joy and terror of that time. The glory of God and the cruelty of man, which at the age of 8 she had experienced all in the same day.
> ➤ She remembered wanting to share in her sister's 16th surprise birthday

party, and learning she was not wanted.

➤ She remembered her Confirmation at the age of 14 and her initial determination NEVER to marry and to become a nun and then meeting Hunter who made that determination fade into the shadows.

➤ She remembered learning that her favorite Uncle was dying of heart disease and sending a decorated pine tree to his funeral which occurred days before Christmas. He loved Christmas so. For some reason she could not fathom that "funeral arrangement", had angered her adopted mother greatly, which broke Liz's heart even more and drove her spirit further inward.

- ➢ She remembered learning of her godmother's death; three days after it had occurred and feeling the pain that had never left her from not being able to say good bye. Her mother had told her it was to "protect her" but all it did was hurt her.

- ➢ She thought of her wedding night with Hunter and the joy comingled with the sadness and fear.

- ➢ She thought of the 5 babies she had lost to miscarriage and the emptiness it still left in her heart and waiting arms.

- She remembered the birth of her three children and the absolute joy of the family she had so longed for
- She thought of the morning she found him cold and curled up in a fetal position, looking like a small boy on the day he died.
- She remembered the hatred in her children's voices…
- She thought and she cried endless tears that she thought would not end. And she softened… as the wall around her heart began to crumble

THE WEDDING CEREMONY

The Apache Wedding Prayer

"Now you will feel no rain,
For each of you will be shelter to the other.
Now you will feel no cold,
For each of you will be warmth to the other.
Now there is no more loneliness,
For each of you will be companion to the other.
Now you are two bodies,
But there is one life before you.
Go now to your dwelling place,
To enter into the days of your togetherness.
And may your days be good and long upon the earth."

One early spring morning, Elizabeth noted that a young couple were being watched and discussed with sly smiles and winks among the tribe. When she asked Lolotea what was going on, she laughed in her tinkling laugh and said; "A wedding".

"Oh", said Liz. "That is wonderful! When is the ceremony? May I attend?"

Again, Lolotea giggled in that lilting tone and said. "No, they are already married"

"You see, when an Apache girl has reached the second year of her puberty the fact is widely circulated, and all present are invited to a grand feast and dance. She is then deemed marriageable and open to the solicitations of the young warriors. On such occasions the girl is dressed in all her finery. Small bells are hung to the skirts of her buckskin robe and along the sides of her high moccasins, which reach the knee. Bits of tinsel are profusely scattered all over her clothing, until she is fairly weighed down by the quantity of her ornaments. Meat in abundance is cooked, and the guests partake of it until they have had their fill. Twilt-kah-yee, an intoxicating beverage is freely distributed. A dried ox-hide is laid upon the ground, and some of the more noted musicians entertain the company with improvised songs, while others beat time upon the ox-hide with long and tough sticks. The noise of this drumming can be heard for two miles on a clear, calm night."

"Old warriors meet and recount their exploits while the younger men ogle and court the marriageable girls. The old women delight in cooking the supper and furnishing it to their hungry guests."

"Suddenly a shout is raised, and a number of young men, variously attired in the skins of buffalo, deer, cougars, bears, and other beasts, each looking as nearly natural as possible, make their appearance, and commence dancing to a regular beat around a huge central fire. The women pretend to be greatly alarmed at this irruption of beasts; the men seize their weapons and brandish them with menacing gestures, to which the human menagerie pays no sort of attention. Finding their efforts to intimidate futile, they lay aside their arms and join in the dance, which is then made more enjoyable by the intermingling of the young girls."

"In the meantime the one in whose honor all these rejoicings are given, remains isolated in a huge lodge, in which are assembled the saga mores and principal warriors of the tribe. She is not allowed to participate in, or even see what is going on outside; but listens patiently to the responsibilities of her marriageable condition. This feast lasts from three to five days, according to the wealth of the girl's father. After it is finished she is divested of her eyebrows, which is intended to publish the fact that she is in the matrimonial market. A month afterward the eyelashes are pulled out, one by one, until no a hair remains."

This greatly troubled Elizabeth, and the reasons for this extraordinary despoliation Liz was not able to learn, and she doubted much if the Apaches themselves could assign any cause to the act beyond that of tradition. Apparently, no arguments could induce them to stop the practice. It probably arose from a desire to look unlike any other people, and to add to their ferociousness of aspect. All Liz knew for sure is that is looked painful as hell and she was grateful that it was NOT part of her engagement or marriage ceremonies.

"Hell", she thought while being told of this ceremony, "I don't even pluck my own damned eyebrows. OUCH!"

Lolotea continued by stating that "Apache girls are wholly free in their choice of husbands. Parents never attempt to impose suitors upon their acceptance, and the natural coquetry of the sought-for bride is allowed full scope. These are their halcyon days, for after marriage comes the deluge."

"The deluge? Why a deluge?" asked Liz.

"Patience and you will understand", she replied.

"Any amount of ogling, sly pressing of hands, stolen interviews, etc., is gone through with, until the brave believes his "game made." Then he proceeds to test his actual standing, which is invariably done as follows:"

"In the night time he stakes his horse in front of her wikiup, via a few slender branches, with their butt ends in the ground and their tops bound together. The suitor then retires and awaits the decision. Should the girl favor the suitor, his horse is taken by her, led to water, fed, and secured in front of **his** lodge; but should she decline the proffered honor, she will pay no attention to the suffering steed. Four days comprise the term allowed her for an answer in the manner related. A ready acceptance is apt to be criticized with some severity, while a tardy one is regarded as the extreme of coquetry. Scarcely any of them will lead the horse to water before the second day, as a hasty performance of that act would indicate an unusual desire to be married; nor will any suffer the fourth day to arrive without furnishing the poor animal with its requisite food and drink, provided they intend to accept the suitor, for such a course would render them liable to the charge of excessive vanity."

Lolotea said, "In your world, the possession of gold and silver indicates success and wealth; I believe much to your people's detriment. Gold and silver are the recognized mediums of exchange for your goods, and are the basis of your monetary system; but with the Apache a horse is money, and the value of any thing is regulated by the number of horses which it may bring. Of course, the animal must be sound, and not over ten years of age, and no blacksmith or horse trader is more skillful in these matters than the Apache!"

"The lover, having been accepted, now has the duty to determine how many horses her parents are willing to receive for their daughter; it being mutually understood that the animals are given as a recompense for her services to the family. In exact proportion to the number of horses given, her worth and attractiveness are exalted. If a girl is sold for one animal, no matter how good she may actually be, she is deemed of little account--quite plebeian, and by no means of the societal best--by the rest of those present."

Elizabeth now felt sure that our modern expression, "a one-horse affair," took its origin from this Apache system of graduated values.

"On the third night of the feasting and celebrating prior to the marriage, the bride and bridegroom suddenly disappear. During the whole of the time mentioned, they have been constantly in the presence of the sachems and wise women of the tribe, and are never permitted to even speak with each other. But love is far more watchful than precaution, and when the old people are overcome by drowsiness, incident upon long wakefulness and frequent imbibing of fermented beverages, the young couple manage to make their escape, usually with the connivance of their seniors, who pretend to be quite innocent of the matter."

"Several days prior to his marriage the bridegroom selects some beautiful and retired spot, from three to five miles from the main camp, and there he erects one of the shelters already described, but festooned with wild flowers, and generally embowered among the trees in a place difficult to discover. There he retreats with his bride, a sufficiency of provision having been laid in to last them a week or ten days, and there they take up their temporary abode. Their absence is expected, and re-appearance creates no visible recognition, as it is deemed indelicate to make any open demonstration on such occasions. This is what you, Elizabeth, are now witnessing. This is what you call the end of their honeymoon. The young bride assumes the air and pretenses of extraordinary modesty, and in the event of meeting one of her former associates, invariably turns her back or hides her face.

"In a week, this seeming bashfulness gives place to the regular and arduous duties of the Apache wife, and her life of toil and slavish suffering commences; the deluge.""

The warrior may at any time repudiate his conjugal companion, and her chances for a second marriage consist in her reputation as a good worker, or for her personal attractions. In either case, she experiences no difficulty in obtaining a second, and even a third or fourth husband, but her market depends upon her prominence in these respects."

Elizabeth learned, from Noch-Del-Kline, that should there be any children, it becomes the reputed father's duty to provide for their support, and he, in turn, imposes that responsibility upon his other wives. The women are by no means averse to sharing the affections of their lords with other wives, as the increased number lessens the work for each individual, but the place of honor is always assigned to the one whom was married first, irrespective of age.

The custom of polygamy was not always in vogue among the Apaches. A celebrated warrior, and one wise in the traditions of his people, Noch-de-Klinne told Liz that there was a time when only one woman was deemed the proper share of one man, but their losses by war and other causes, had so reduced the number of males that it was judged politically correct to make a change in this custom. It was deemed necessary for the survival of the Apache

He further added, that he thought degeneracy had been produced by its adoption, and that the individuals of the tribe had become alienated from each other and from the Creator.

"I, myself, rejoice in but one wife with whom I have lived since I was twenty moons, and", he said "although she has fallen into the sere and yellow leaf, I prefer her to all the young and more attractive women."

"My wife has had borne me two fine sons and a daughter, all of whom are alive and well, and she possesses the experience requisite to make me a contented husband. My oldest son is a warrior, and my best friend and confidant."

Noch-Del-Klinne deprecated the system of polygamy, and thought that it would eventually emasculate and destroy the independence of his tribe. His views were fully seconded by several other elders but, despite their wisdom and "magic" they could not hold their own against the practices of Ka-e-te-nay, Itza-chu, and other prominent and more licentious and younger men of the tribe... and so their society had fallen from grace in the Shaman's eyes and so too, he believed, in Usen's

After her long chat with Lolotea and Noch De Klinne, Elizabeth wandered back to her pallet in the back of the cave and lay down lost in memory. She looked out through the opening of the cave and watched the stars pepper the velvet sky until finally she found what she was looking for – ORION! She had always felt, since Hunter had died, that his spirit resided on the belt of that constellation and whenever it finally appeared above the gate of her townhome, she felt safe and at ease... for a little while. Now, how she needed to feel that way again. As tears silently and gently fell down her cheeks, Ranger, no longer a puppy, stole up to her side and licked her tenderly before laying his head in her lap and sighing.

Hello YOU, she whispered into his velvet satellite ear. You always know when I really need you, Ranger... but what I don't think you know is that I ALWAYS Need YOU... and love you so." Ranger whimpered gently and nuzzled her cheek.

"You would have liked Hunter, Ranger... and I know he would have liked you. I miss him so... We were married 24 years before he died. 24 years... "

With that, Elizabeth fell into a dream filled sleep with Ranger sleeping cradled in her arm...

In her dreams, she was a young girl of 18 again and it was the morning of her wedding day. Her bridesmaids had all arrived and her sister was bustling around the upstairs trying "to help" and asking her if she was "nervous"

"Not a bit, Dianne", she had said. "In fact, this is the first thing I have done in my life that I am absolutely certain of. Oh, I know mother and daddy don't like him. I know YOU don't like him and perhaps you all have very good reasons. But I just know his heart, and his soul and his smile and it will be okay. I will MAKE it all okay"

Her father, waiting for her downstairs, took her by the hand as they prepared to head out to the car and take the short drive to the church. "It's not too late to change your mind. It would be okay with you Mom and me if you don't want to go through with this."

She had kissed him gently on the cheek and said "No, Daddy. I am not changing my mind. I love Hunter. I know you don't, but I do."

They were married in the Catholic Cathedral of her hometown... the one where she had almost decided to take vows in when she felt she so wanted to become a nun. Mother Superior taught her that the convent was not the place for her to be as she was trying to hide from life. Mother Superior had been right! "In my own way, thought Liz, I am still trying to hide."

The ceremony had been beautiful, her colors of pink and purple were perfect for the late summer wedding. Her gown, old fashioned and laden with pearls and silk and lace had a long following veil with a Juliet cap. She had carried a bouquet of daisies with white roses and oh how handsome Hunter had looked waiting for her at the altar.

When the ceremony and mass had concluded, they walked down the aisle as husband and wife to the song "We've Only Just Begun". It was the beginning of a brand new way of life for her.

Brand new, and yet frighteningly exactly the same...

A WOMAN'S VALUE

"The first man holds it in his hands
He holds the sun in his hands
In the center of the sky, he holds it in his hands
As he holds it in his hands, it starts upward.
The first woman holds it in her hands
She holds the moon in her hands
In the center of the sky, she holds it in her hands
As she holds it in her hands, it starts upward.
Now the Mother Earth
And the Father Sky
Meeting, joining one another,
Helpmates ever, they."

~Navajo prayer~

One day an Apache woman died in the camp, and Elizabeth asked Noch-Del-Klinne if there would be great mourning and a funeral.

He simply smiled at the idea, and replied: "She was a woman; her death is of no account."

"Of no account?" responded Elizabeth somewhat angrily. "She was a living member of your tribe! You seem to honor and revere Lolotea and even your own wife, but now tell me that this woman is of no importance? I thought you respected all life?"

The Shaman smiled patiently at her and said very calmly; "Lolotea is NOT of this world and can never die. She is the daughter of Usen. However, I and other members of this tribe, although some are very old and ancient, will eventually face death in the mortal world as the Great Creator decides.

"As to my wife, yes, little one, I would indeed mourn her, but a woman's importance to her family and her tribe are honored in her life. In death, she no longer holds importance. A warrior, however, is honored for giving his life for his tribe."

As Elizabeth went over to the body of the dead woman to say a little prayer and to offer her condolences, several other women of the tribe formed a wall to prevent her from getting too close. Sadly, Elizabeth learned that the Apache were extremely reserved about letting outsiders approach their dead, and invariably buried them under the cover of night, with the most cautious secrecy.

Elizabeth did learn that their dead were conveyed to the most convenient height, and deposited in the ground, care being taken to shroud their bodies with stones as to prevent the wolves and coyotes from digging them up and mutilating their remains. Everything the dead had possessed was scrupulously placed in the grave, but with what ceremonies, and under what observances, she was never to discover.

Unlike the death of the woman, which was almost unnoticed except by her intimate friends and personal female relatives, she was told that the death of a warrior provoked an excessive demonstration of woe and a general sense of serious loss.

"So, Elizabeth asked, "that woman's relatives are not permitted to keep a single memory of her? Something to hold onto?"

Noch-Del-Klinne, again smiled wisely and said "the reason why we bury all the worldly goods of dead people with their bodies, is because of a strange disease which broke out among our people several years before I was even born, and carried off great numbers of the tribe. The deaths were horribly painful and nothing the Medicine man had in his power could stop it. It was found that to use the clothing or household property of the deceased, or to come in contact with such a person, was almost certain to result in a like sickness to the individual doing these things. That was when they passed a law to bury with him or her every single thing that the deceased possessed at the time of death, and all that he or she might have used or touched before that event."

Elizabeth opened her mouth to ask more questions but she felt his mind snap shut. He strictly forbore telling her anything more, although Liz made every effort to draw him out on several occasions.

Elizabeth finally realized that the disease the Shaman had alluded to was the smallpox; for there was plenty of evidence that it had raged among the

Apaches in some past period and that is was brought to a virgin country from the white settlers.

"No wonder they won't let me near their dead... I am white!"

Suddenly, all of this talk of death and ceremonies dissolved her into a puddle of tears... memories, long kept at bay, overwhelmed her. Memories of the day Hunter died, the demand he had left her with that no ceremony of any kind be held... her lack of support from children or friends to even allow her to mourn...

LESSONS

Oh, Great Spirit

Whose voice I hear in the winds,

And whose breath gives life to all the world,

Hear me, I am small and weak.

I need your strength and wisdom.

Let me walk in beauty and make my eyes ever behold

The red and purple sunset.

Make my hands respect the things you have

Made and my ears sharp to hear your voice.

Make me wise so that I may understand the things

You have taught your people.

Let me learn the lesson you have

Hidden in every leaf and rock."

~ Chief Yellow Lark ~

For days upon days both before and after getting to witness or take part in the tribe's rituals and customs, Elizabeth studied and worked as she had never studied and worked before in her life. She spent hours every day at the feet of Noch-Del-Klinne repeating chants, correcting her speech, going over and over difficult phrases. The old mystic sometimes laid aside his work and led her in a chant, almost as if he were a music master, but often he just went on with his own work. The old man would lapse into hours of uninterrupted teaching of old handed down legends. The Apache of the modern world did not often share their stories with outsiders -- but here, in this land of in between, Elizabeth was being told all. She had grown to love this man with reverence and respect. They laughed a great deal as well, as the old man was filled with humor which he shared liberally.

At night, when Lolotea was not playing or walking with him, Ranger came and slept by Elizabeth and would nuzzle her... licking her mending legs and arms; letting her know that he loved her still. One such night, Elizabeth took out her old bandanna and wrapped half of the broken arrowhead inside of it and then wrapped it around Ranger's neck. She took the larger piece, wrapped a leather chord around it, and then hung it around her own neck.

She whispered into his big, soft, satellite ears, "these two pieces together make us whole, and one day soon, we will always be together again in a world free from pain, immorality, or cruelty. Remember, you are my Ranger... MY Ranger. You are my fur boy!"

Ranger leaned in to give her his version of a hug and she grabbed his neck tightly and sobbed deeply into his soft fur for several minutes.

"You are all I have left boy.... just you."

Ranger crawled up onto her, trying to be the lap dog he thought he was, and stayed with her until she fell asleep.

During the course of her training, Elizabeth was told that there were many surprises in store for her while she dwelled here within the Superstition and to keep an open mind. She was assured that she would receive the inner sight to accept those things and not to allow doubts and shock to preclude this receiving guidance. She was told that she would be allowed to experience a special meeting that had been set up by the Great Creator.

One night, Noch-Del-Klinne explained; "Great knowledge will be opened up and truths presented which cannot be disclaimed by the masses of human entities, the time has drawn nigh for your meeting of the highest universal energies of the Great Creator. It is a special and rare gift to be granted to you"

"The changes you will be navigating, he continued, will help you to awaken to a deeper expression of your soul's path. You are a light bearer, Elizabeth. You were chosen to incarnate in this time and place to help bring more peace and love into your spirit and thereby into your world. This, your journey of healing, has the potential to be of great service to others who are going through similar experiences."

"Be BRAVE!"

Elizabeth wanted to pursue the subject, but Noch-Del-Klinne had turned his mind off and she knew no more discussion would take place that night.

As the lessons drew to a close, the old wise one placed a calm hand on her shoulder and said, "Remember, my daughter, with faith anything is possible".

One day, following a lesson which had been of such a strong spiritual nature that she was exhausted from thinking on them, Elizabeth became restless. During this lesson Noch-Del-Klinne had firmly told her "We Apache believe in Diye; the "power inherent within all animals, plants and humans." We rely on our animal brothers and sisters for everything including food, clothing, transportation, agriculture and seasonal changes."

"They also serve as teachers, companions and spiritual guides. For you, there is a connection with this animal in some form. Every human being has at least one power animal which is either chosen or given to them. In your case there are two such animals, this dog and the hawk. These animals will be with you for life in both the natural and spiritual world. Do not spurn their guidance! Listen to the animals."

Since it was far too early for Ranger to come and spend time with her, she did what she had not done since being brought into this land of in between – she went looking for him.

Her legs and hip fractures had healed, although still painful, and with the aid of a walking staff, her walks had become quite long. As she had always done on the "other side of the mountains", she enjoyed her time spent in the out of doors. Her arm was almost healed and she was able to use it without discomfort for some tasks. Her teeth however... well nothing could be done about those here now. Over all, she felt extremely well for what she had endured.

As she strolled along the valley floor, she noticed a side canyon that had not come to her attention before. She usually walked with Ranger during these breaks away from the tribe, so decided that maybe she had been too involved with him to have noticed. It was a short canyon and at the head of the valley was a particularly beautiful alcove, the cliffs sheltering and rounding behind a fin or rock jutting out form the canyon wall into which the ages had carved a sandstone arch. The front of the arch rested in a high rock buttress, a butte that was crowned form the level of the arch top by a thin, cone-like spire that reached several feet into the air. At the foot of the butte, under the arch, the floods of bygone years had left a level plain of some yards in diameter which looked almost like a stage. A water fall flowed behind it. There had also been some spectacular petroglyphs scattered along the cliff walls as she passed along the trail.

Suddenly Elizabeth was stopped in stunned disbelief. From behind the arch, a gossamer clad maiden appeared and leaped to the top of the arch, trailing a segment of living rainbow several yards in length; like a gymnast would do in a ribbon dance. She flung the gauzy membrane into the air and it furled and floated above her as if immune to gravity.

The scene in itself was enough to boggle her mind but, still staring with unblinking eyes, she collapsed on a small ledge jutting out beside her; she was staring into the eyes of Dahteste; the young woman whom she had met during the Sunrise Ceremony. (Somehow, Elizabeth felt they had met long before that). Before she could think, a second maiden sprang out to meet Dahteste; she too carried a swirling rainbow section. The second dancer was Lolotea and Elizabeth went numb...

"What can be happening?" her rational mind screamed.

NO SIGNS

"Everything on earth has a purpose,
Every disease an herb to cure it
And every person a mission.
This is the Indian Theory of Existence."
~Mourning Dove~

The morning headlines for the East Valley
Tribune boldly proclaimed: "Teams
Wednesday evening called off their search
for a local writer/poet from Mesa,who
went missing two weeks ago in the
Superstition Mountains. Elizabeth Reed,

aged 58, who has hiked the various trails over the Superstition for the last 16 years went out hiking with her pet shepherd two weeks ago. A good friend of hers reported her as missing around 10:30 p.m. that night when he had not received any word from her for the entire day.

An extensive search has been made for Ms. Reed and any sign of her dog over the course of the past four weeks; to no avail. Due to the extremely high temperatures, the monsoon rains and high winds, it is the conclusion of the Pinal County Sheriff's Department and their Search and Rescue Team that the chance of her survival after all of this time is unlikely."

Jon had been told the night before by Steve Wilson, a member of the Search and Rescue team: "Our search won't continue on any official basis, unless we find some evidence that warrants us being out there. I am so very sorry, Mr. Nickels, but we honestly feel that we haven't left any stone unturned."

"Unofficially, Mr. Nickels", he said as he placed a comforting hand on his shoulder... "We will never stop looking for her. We NEVER really give up. But, please don't hold out too much hope that when we do find her, that she will be alive."

Jon felt a wave of nausea pass over him as he let himself crumble onto the hood of

Elizabeth's jeep. Jimmy Dale, tears in his eyes, sat beside him on the bumper.

"You are giving up!!!" said Jon in absolute disbelief. "No body? No sign of anything out of place? You will just leave her out here?" "Alone?"

"We are truly sorry, Mr. Nickels. If, at any time, some real evidence comes to the surface, believe me, we will open the case and search again, for now, we have done everything we can possibly do. We have had the helicopters out, men and women on horseback, cadaver dogs, and almost 200 people combing the trails and cliffs for two weeks. We can't find a single sign of her. As much as I know you want to believe otherwise, there is no way anyone could survive this long out here in this weather; even if she was uninjured."

"My prayers are with you, Sir. I am so sorry for your loss."

Jon's mind was reeling. What was he supposed to do now? Everything in him said that Elizabeth was out there and very much alive. He looked at Jimmy Dale who seemed to be thinking the same thing.

"Jon, you and I will keep searching every spare moment. I, too, believe her spirit is very much alive and out here in this mountain"

THE RITUAL

"When a vision comes from the thunder beings of the west, it comes with terror like a thunder storm; but when the storm of vision has passed, the world is greener and happier; for wherever the truth of vision comes upon the world, it is like a rain. The world, you see, is happier after the terror of the storm"
~Chapter 16:Heyoka Ceremony~.

Stunned by this appearance of what seemed to be actual "spirits" Elizabeth stared in absolute amazement. Just as suddenly, Dahteste and Lolotea were joined by five other maidens who, to Elizabeth, also appeared as spirit forms; although even more so. Each had a rainbow section, and the air of the canyon walls seemed to shimmer and radiate with veils of vibrant color. Muted flute music with rolling thunder guided and timed the swirling and twirling dance of the spirit maidens. Following Dahteste, the company made a circle around the top of the alcove, the rainbows floating, furling, and coiling in the space above the alcove. The music picked up a beat, as the dancers again landed in the arch, and the music changed into a triumphal march, dominated now by drums of some sort.

The dancers suddenly drew in the streamers and then reissued them in gigantic flashing pom-pom like flowers. Every frond of every flower flickered and flashed as the maidens gyrated, pirouetted, turned cartwheels and jumped back and forth on the arch tip in a frenzy of controlled maneuvers, the flowers sweeping up, around and below the arch until there was an effect of pulsing radiance shooting out in every direction like the bursting of multicolored fireworks in the sky. In one final exuberant gesture, the spirit dancers cast the flowers high in to the air and, turning back into rainbow streamers, drew them back in. Dahteste was the central dancer and it appeared as if this might be some sort of ritual lesson, more shared than taught.

Down again onto the floor of the alcove they tumbled, drawing in the rainbows. Then in a whirling-dervish pirouette, they cast them up where they flared like a cloud of smoke, the free and flickering ends licking like flames of lightning in a multicolored fire.

The canyon seemed to darken until Elizabeth had the feeling it was night. As the dancers whirled in the alcove they were suddenly joined by two men from either side of the arch. The men were dressed in bleached buckskin. Dahteste and the two men proceeded to perform a most spectacular dance and after a few minutes Lolotea joined the three. Elizabeth suddenly felt sure she knew one of the male dancers... and her concern grew... the emotions of this experience becoming more than she felt she could handle.

She continued to stare in amazement as the remaining spirit maidens rejoined those on the out cropped ledge and the five additional male dancers joined the fray. The girls drew their steamers into scarves and filled the canyon with flashes of flickering light far more intense than Saint Elmo's fire, even if only brief flashes.

The dancers flung up the sections of rainbow into the sky. As the music changed and fell into a sensuous beat,

they manipulated the cobweb like clouds

into golden poppies, taller than

themselves, and Elizabeth noticed their

costumes had changed and were now

iridescent silver with gold trim. The

poppies did not seem to touch the floor

but they bent, swayed and twirled, lifting

and swinging the beautiful dancers whose

graceful movements swayed and flashed

to the beat of the music. The metallic

poppies seemed to somehow support, to

enfold, to lift and display them. Then,

Elizabeth realized, that the poppies were

actually men and the levitation an

illusion. Elizabeth could not help but

think that even the stars in the sky must

sway to this beauty and know that these

dancers belonged to them.

"Kokopelli? Star people? How can this be real?" she thought

The drumbeat then changed once more and it was as if Elizabeth had caught a warning, a feeling of disaster in the thunder, a foretelling of doom. Dahteste and Lolotea were somehow changed into yellow spider-web wrapped forms. Towing their rainbow which seemed to have grown heavy into position, they turned apart and perched on the farther canyon rims opposite each other. The other dancers sank still circling, and the sweet aroma and moistness of the air sank with them.

As she watched Dahteste and Lolotea
spread their arms, holding the rainbow in
their fingertips, pulled it taught, flipped it
a couple of time, and flung it into the sky.
The drums screamed in protest. The
rainbow arched up like a ripple in a pool,
and disappeared as the drums stopped
mid-beat. Silence was absolute.
Movement Ceased. Only the hawk circling
above continued its endless glide across
the silence of the heavens.

Elizabeth sat in wonder, oblivious to
everything around her; she failed to even
notice the arm which was placed across
her shoulder from behind. Her being still
throbbed to the beat of the drums, her
mind filled with flashes of half formed
ideas which tumbled in an incoherent

kaleidoscope. Gradually her body quieted and her mind began to find its focus once again.

Suddenly she could comprehend the message the Shaman had given her; that she must purify herself, purge herself of this mortality and become pure spirit to be able to move into the beyond through the Sipapu. To obtain that excellence, she realized, she must undergo a metamorphosis as complete as a chrysalis produces a butterfly from the larvae.

The Ultimate Answer?

Oh, Great Spirit
Whose voice I hear in the winds
And whose breath gives life to all the world,
Hear me, I am small and weak.
I need your strength and wisdom.
Let me walk in beauty and make my eyes ever behold
The red and purple sunset.
Make my hands respect the things you have
Made and my ears sharp to hear your voice.
Make me wise so that I may understand the things
That you have taught your people.
Let me learn the lessons you have
Hidden in every leaf and rock
I seek strength, not to be greater than my brother,
But to fight my greatest enemy – myself
Make me always ready to come to you
With clean hands and straight eyes.
So when life fades, as the fading sunset
My Spirit may come to you without shame.
~ Chief Yellow Lark ~

Death? Death was one answer, but there had to be an alternative. To believe that was the only way was over simplification. Her earthly being was overcome and yet, intuitively, she knew she had moved into a higher spiritual existence. She would gladly die for her beloved shepherd, who had become her only family, but that did not seem to be the solution. Besides, why would Lolotea and her tribe have gone to all the trouble to heal her if she were meant to die here?

Both Nana and Noch-Del-Klinne had told her that anything was possible with faith, but she knew her faith didn't include letting control of her circumstances completely out of her own hands. Did it? Death was surely a new beginning in her book but she also believed that one died ONLY when one's time came and not before; and never was it acceptable to die by any controlled method.

Once when she was about 12, she tried to take the most precious gift that God had given her and throw it away... a suicide attempt that luckily went wrong; it left a small scar on her right wrist which she would look at whenever her life took desperate turns.

Many were the times during her marriage to her beloved Hunter which, though filled with love was fraught with drug addiction, alcoholism and tears, and then often after his death that she had begged God to let her come home; to let her die.

"No, not actual death." Elizabeth knew that only God had the right to make that decision. But oh, how she longed to join those she loved -- maybe on the other side thru the Sipapu she would find peace?

One thing that Elizabeth was convinced of by her experience with the after effects of watching the dance was that unless she divested herself of this earthly "humanness" -- her mortality-- she could never attain the level of Lolotea; even if she did go through the Sipapu with her. She carefully reviewed what the Shaman had told her remembering that with faith anything was possible.

She felt that there was a slim chance that she could still purify herself with meditation and prayer; and she was as ready as she ever would be to give it a try.

Elizabeth turned around to look for Ranger... knowing that tomorrow she would go alone into the mountains and make herself ready to travel to the other side to be with him and the tribe. But Ranger was not there. Instead, as she turned, she looked directly into the eyes of her beloved Hunter.

Shock turned the world black as Elizabeth collapsed to the ground.

A WALK WITH THE PAST

"My life will be forever autumn, cause you're not here."
~Moody Blues

Suddenly, in a haze of fog, she found
herself back in her own time... but far
back in her own time. She was fourteen...

In the years prior to her fourteenth birthday, she could not recall a great deal of joy, tenderness, or love. Oh, she did find those things from time to time in the faces of her Uncle Bill, and her Godmother Lucy. However, the times she had with them were far too short, so she had learned to survive in a climate of anger and sadness by keeping the world at bay. After she turned fourteen, however, she met the first man who would change so much of her life...

The young man, who was seventeen when they began dating in the spring of that year, shortly before she turned 15, was Hunter. In the early fall of that same year, he arrived at her parent's home on a Saturday morning and told her he was taking her on a picnic. He would not, however, divulge their destination. She cuddled up beside him as he drove the old Scout Jeep to a "special place", and enjoyed the aroma of the fried chicken he had just picked up on his way to get her from Kentucky Fried Chicken; it smelled wonderful.

They entered the town limits and drove through it without blinking; as to do so would have meant missing the entire town. Just as they started to exit the town limits, Hunter turned off onto a dead-end road.

About one half mile down the road,

he stopped and parked in front of a

large wrought iron fence and gate.

The gate was opened wide.

About one quarter of a mile inside

those gates was a large tranquil

pond on which beautiful white swans

glided in peaceful majesty. This was

the place they went to picnic; a place
called "Smith's Pond".

The leaves had already begun to turn
russet, gold, red, orange and yellow.
The grass, which surrounded the
pond was a thick and soft as a shag
carpet.

She immediately sat down and took
off her shoes. Laughing, Hunter did
the same and they walked in the
grass amid the few leaves that had
already fallen, waded in the cold
pond, and fed the swans with the old
bread Hunter had thoughtfully
brought with him.

Not prone to showing much emotion, Hunter had to ask Liz if she were happy?

Happy? Oh more than happy. This place was ripped right out of a fairy tale, she said. It's like you stepped right into one of my dreams and ripped this place of peace right out of them."

On that day, Hunter taught Elizabeth to trust him and to love him... the love would remain for eternity but trust is a fragile thing.

"For a man shall leave his mother; a woman leaves her home. They shall travel on to where the two shall be as one..." ~ John Denver

The music and words as performed by Peter Paul and Mary now came flooding into her brain. Suddenly she was a young bride of 18 walking up the aisle to become united with a handsome 20-year-old groom; Hunter. The wedding was huge and beautiful but not the wedding she and Hunter had planned. They had wanted something a little (well a lot) more simple.... Out in an apple orchard with Hunter in jeans and a wedding shirt and Liz in a muslin gown with a crown of orange blossoms on her head. But, years ago she had promised her mother that this day would be hers... and so it was.

For the next twenty-three years,

those words continued to ring true

as they grew closer together, built a

family, celebrated the joys of success,

and found solutions to life's

upheavals while working together as

one viable unit. Everything they did,

they did as one and Elizabeth had

believed that, so long as they were

together, nothing could ever defeat

them.

Military separation did not defeat

them, for their spirits were always

united across the ocean miles

.

The diagnosis of their youngest son's

brain damage did not defeat them as

they took their love and surrounded

him in its cocoon.

Illness did not defeat them, as she

suffered miscarriages, MS, throat

cancer, and breast cancer. The drug

addiction that began to consume

him. The heart attacks and

subsequent open heart surgery that

seemingly destroyed his will to live.

Addiction... addiction became the

enemy at the door. The one neither

could seem to battle. The war they

both lost. The blow that took the

very breath from him and sealed her

in a living tomb.

Just as they had made the decision to leave the dream home that had somehow turned into a nightmare, Hunter was diagnosed with arteriosclerosis disease and congestive heart failure after undergoing open heart surgery at the age of 37,

Then when he was 43, reality hit her like a sledge hammer. Chameleon like, she watched his skin change color from pink, to ash-gray, to the color of starched hospital linen. Earlier the external tissues had begun to take on water that the pump could no longer remove, over flowing the banks of the heart with toxins. Suddenly, a vacuum sucked

the oxygen from the room, and the
death squeeze began again.

Placing his body on a thin, metal
table in a room maintained at meat
cutter's temperatures, they plugged
it into electric monitors, painfully
piercing it with three needles
connected to two plastic and one
glass bottle, as they talked and
laughed; impervious to the death
stalk and to her fear.

Prayers went out and rosary beads
worked in hands grown older as she
stood, once again, at the gates of
widowhood, too young, still too
young. She longed to rip the pump
that tortured her love form its cage

and strangle it with her own bare hands. She longed to hold the body she loved, tenderly, and caress it until it hurt no more, but gently slept.

Her courage that day held, waned, and held again as the infant day began amid instruments of steel, winter white walls, and medicinal smells. While better living through chemistry, and not the healthy choices she wanted him to make, brought sleep and respite from his excruciating pain and pressure.

Sitting alone at a distance, beside a window filtering light into a room of shadows, she read poetry, prayed, *planned, and then watched in gratitude and love as deep set green eyes in a placid face opened wide and smiled at her. The heart she loved still beat like a metronome and time was still theirs to share. Until a little over a year later... when her world came to an end.*

"I couldn't save you... I couldn't save you" she murmured over and over again as she slowly came out of the stupor of shock.

Opening her eyes, she again gazed into Hunter's and her tears began to fall as she sobbed and her body shook uncontrollably. He was cradling her in his arms and looking down at her so lovingly. Staring up into his face, she noticed that Hunter had not aged. In fact, he now showed no signs of the heart problems, the bloating, or the addiction. He was young... like he was 30 and wearing the white wedding shirt she so loved to see him in.

"How? How is this possible? Is it real?" she whispered.

Smiling that little boy smile of his that she so loved... he said "Yes, Liz... it's real and I **am** here. Truth is, baby, I have always been here; always and forever will be. But honey, it's long past time that you let ME go..."

"Let you go?", she almost shouted as she came to a sitting position. "No, Hunter, that will never happen! I don't want to let you go and I don't want to have anyone else in my life but you; not really. So much was left unsaid and undone in our lives. Then there was the shattering of our family – you know the children hate me. They know so little of our life together; the things I did to protect you; all of you. I keep wanting to tell them, but I don't want to shatter their love and memories of you." Her sobs began anew.

"I don't want to shatter my love and memories of you. I tried to be a good wife, and a good mother. I wanted to save you, Hunter. I failed."

"All I do is fail."

He smiled that wonderful smile, his hazel eyes shining in a face so much younger then hers now. "Stop it now! You were a very good wife and you did not fail. My troubles were not about you or even the children... the burden was mine; then and now."

"Something that I have learned now, too late for the life I lived with you and the kids, is that we cannot save one another no matter how much we want to. Nor can we hold the love of another captive, be it husband, wife, child or friend. That is up to each individual and the path they have chosen. We meet others in our life as the Great Spirit requires; to test us, to teach us, and to guide us. If we fail to listen and learn... the fault is only our own and we cannot blame others. "

"Nor Liz, can any one person assume the blame or the control over another person's actions. If you had or still have any fault, it is in this area; thinking you can control the decisions, actions, words, etc. of another person."

"Come now and let's walk. Lolotea has prepared a picnic for us down by the stream. I was listening to your thoughts as you "slept" and remember well our first picnic together and she was more than happy to have the women of the tribe help to make this a special day. Let's enjoy this time that has been given to us."

Hunter took Elizabeth's hand in his and gently pulled her to her feet. Then she felt his arms surrounding her in the big bear hug she so loved and caught the scent of Aramis... "Cologne Hunter? Here?" She looked up at him questioningly.

He softly laughed and said, "Only in memory Liz. As right now, I smell "Wind Song" on you. The strongest memories are what stay with us and for each of us; one of those memories is a special scent. "

As he led her down to the Indian blanket
that was placed on the bank of the stream
and hollowed bowls of fruits, flat corn
bread, and fresh gourds of water placed
upon it, he leaned down and gently kissed
her and slowly and deliberately, he took
off the dress she wore. He kissed the
scars that the mastectomy had left

behind; the tears began to flow as her
heart broke open; she became a puddle.

"I'm sorry Hunter, I could not save them;
referring to the breasts he had once so
loved. See I failed"

"Silly old lady of mine. YOU are alive...
that is not failure"

Through her tearful sobs, she let go with a
flurry of questions: "Why, Hunter? Why
did you choose to leave? Why would you
not go into rehab? Why did you tell the
kids some of the things you did? Why
didn't you want to stay with me??"

"Shhhh Liz. Too many why's to which I
have not the wisdom to answer. Just keep

remembering this truth… none of it was because of you OR the children. The responsibility was my own as is the responsibility for the life you have chosen to live since I transcended. As will be the life you choose to live from today forward when you go back."

"Go back? Back through the Sipapu to the other side? Oh Hunter, if it means I get to stay with your forever and have Ranger, I am so ready to cross through and I think I am strong enough to do so. I don't ever want to be separated from you again."

And then she heard words that she had heard after the fall, when she was so near death:

"Not yet, babe. There is still so much for you to see and do."

"Oh my God, Hunter, it was you in that wash with me after I fell? You?"

"Yes, Liz, it was me… and it was Lolotea whom Ranger sensed and went to get. You were never there alone. Now hold on to yourself…and to me", he said squeezing her hand "as you are about to hear a truth."

Elizabeth squeezed his hand tight and looked deeply into his eyes. "What is it?"

"You already crossed through the Sipapu when Lolotea and members of the tribe carried you into the wall of the Mountain.

You left the world we shared together months ago. But now, it is time for you to go back."

She quickly pulled her hand away and glared at him. "What the Hell? So what were all the preparations for when I asked if I could go through the Sipapu? When I said I wanted Ranger to stay with me?"

Gently he said; "To prepare you to go home. You do NOT belong here Liz. There is a life for you to live that for these past many years you have out rightly refused to live... first as my wife, then as the kid's mother, and now as my widow. YOU have not lived an honest life of your own in these more than fifty years and you must before you get to pass through again to stay. "

She fell into his chest, crumpled in defeat; the wind and hope suddenly knocked out of her. "Hunter, I don't want to go back. I don't want to be without you or the kids any more. It has been too hard. I am worn out and I never seem to get it right. Never! The bills, the cancer, the taxes... Nothing goes right!"

Hunter pulled her to him, and in the dying sunlight, on that Indian blanket, gently made love to Liz with a tenderness she had not known even when he was in the land of the living. Her mind opened further and softened, just as her body did to his touch, and tears fell again. Healing tears. Tears of tenderness, and love, and memory.

Hunter dressed and began to build a small campfire as desert nights grow quite cold in the evenings by the end of September and remain that way until May. As the stars began to appear, Liz and Hunter sat by the river, bathed in the campfire's light and warmth, wrapped in one another's arms gazing at an immense star-filled sky. They talked until there were no words left to say and then just held on to one another and Liz fell asleep in with her head in his lap.

Brushing her long hair back from her face, and gently kissing her awake, he pointed up at the heavens, and said: "Orion has arrived, baby. It is time for me to leave now. Remember, hope and love are eternal things and we are never truly apart. No one ever really leaves and we will be together again one day. I will meet you on Brickyard Road. I promise."

She grasped him tightly and kept saying. "No... not again. No! Please."

He stood up and looked down at her and then pointed to a glowing figure standing in the middle of the river under the full moon. It looked like Lolotea and she was holding a golden cage. In the cage was a still beating heart...Liz could hear it beating

On the other side, in shadow -- in mist... she could swear she saw the figure of Jon.

Hunter took her hand and placed it on her chest. Strange, she thought, I don't feel a pulse there? No warmth?

"What is going on, Hunter? What are you trying to say? Please tell me?"

He kissed her, hard, and then said: "This was a dream you had shortly after our baby girl was married; remember? Before you finally released my ashes?"

Elizabeth's mouth fell open.

"Yes, Liz, I was there. As I keep trying to make you understand, I have been close by through everything. I was there when you had the dream and had hoped it would give you the answer I was trying to help you with... so here we are again."

"In that cage beats **your** heart. The one you caged up so tightly when we married and then covered in sack cloth when I died. The one you have since tried to entomb in stone since the children and

life in general added even more grief to
your loss and need of love. "

"In my hand, I hold the key to that cage.
Through the Sipapu awaits Jon and life!
He has never stopped looking for you. Do
I like him? Not really", he laughed; "he's a
bit too pompous for my taste. But what I
do know is that he loves you, and has
taken such good care of you. For that I am
grateful. He has gotten you to be the
young girl I fell in love with once again.
And that is a good thing. It is okay for you
to love him, Liz. I am glad that you do. Let
yourself. Please! "

"So now I give this key to that cage to Jon;
that he can open your heart and you can

live for YOU and end your pain." Saying
that, he tossed the key into the air.

She watched the tiny golden key literally
float through the air and saw a misted
figure reach out to catch it.

With tears in her eyes and understanding
in her heart, she turned to hug Hunter
again; he was gone and Ranger was once
more by her side.

Sinking to her knees, tears streaming
down her face, she hugged his neck tightly
and through choking sobs she said,
"Ranger, it's time to go home boy. Are
you ready to go home?"

Ranger barked his acceptance and tried to lick her tears away.

JOURNEY HOME

"Go forward with courage
When you are in doubt, be still, and wait;
When doubt no longer exists for you, then go forward with
courage.
So long as mists envelop you, be still:
Be still until the sunlight pours through and dispels the mists
As it surely will.
Then act with courage."
~ Chief white Eagle~

Initially, Elizabeth was angry to learn that she and Ranger had actually been on the other side of the Sipapu from the very start. The decision never was whether Ranger would go with Lolotea and leave her behind, the decision was would Ranger return with Liz if she did indeed desired to and was able to do so.

Now, per the purification ceremonies and her walk with the past, she was finally ready to try and Ranger, now a full grown and beautiful dog, was at her side and ready to go with her.

As the sun rose, Noch-Del-Klinne called her to his side.

"The journey ahead of you, back to your place and time, will be a dangerous one", the Shaman gravely told her. As you proceed through the Sipapu show no fear, doubt, or anger. You will find many obstacles in your path but they will be illusion which only faith and belief in yourself will let you cross. "

"What if I fail, wise one? Will I come back here with you and your people?"

"No little one... we will have passed through to the other side ourselves; all except Lolotea and she will return to a higher place to be with her father. You will not see her or us again. Should you fail, you will either die in the attempt or find yourself in another place and time to learn what more you need to do to stand tall in your own time. That choice is now in your hands."

"Have courage! Have faith!"

Lolotea and Dahteste came towards them carrying Elizabeth's backpack with all of its belongings, except the cell phone which had been shattered in her fall so many months ago. They handed these items to Liz and each hugged her in turn.

Then Lolotea presented her with a beautiful pair of red moccasins. "Nana, the Weaver, made these for you; specifically, for your journey home. The Shaman has blessed them. They will help to carry you swiftly and safely.

"We have placed food and water for your journey... enough for you and Ranger. My father, Usen, now alone can carry you the rest of the way. Remember with faith all things are possible"

Lolotea knelt beside Ranger, stroking him lovingly and placed a medicine bag around his neck along with the bandana which held a piece of the broken arrowhead. She kissed him on the forehead and a tear fell from her eye.

"This will protect you, Ranger and help you protect Elizabeth. Never forget what a brave and loving animal spirit you are. Never forget how much you are loved and needed..."

With this, her mind snapped shut and she quickly walked away -- fading into the canyon walls as Elizabeth heard the shriek of a hawk. Dahteste walked over to join Noch-Del-Kline looking bereft...

Liz sat down on the big boulder next to her and slipped into her old torn blue jeans and denim jacket; placing her Apache dress into the pack. Then she put on her new moccasins.

"They fit like a glove Ranger, she said. I wonder how Nana new?" Aren't they lovely boy? What do you think?

Ranger tilted his head and then let out one loud yelp; wagging his tail in total agreement!

Then she made sure her knife and gun were in working order, took note of how much of a water supply she had and slipped into her back pack. A small twinge traveled through her spine and into her right hip; but it was manageable. She still walked with a slight limp and her two fingers on her left hand never healed properly.

Leaning on her walking stick and looking back over her shoulder she waved good-bye to the Shaman and her friend; knowing she would never see them again.

"Well boy", she said to Ranger, let's head off. We must get down through this cave and start heading west to see if we can find our way home; if we will be allowed to go home. First is getting down and then out of this cave... "

First, she came to a Palo Verde tree growing out from the ground in front of the cave. Before the entrance to the cave a lone wolf was stationed; his head lowered and yellow eyes ablaze. Elizabeth paused and remembered the Shaman's words about courage and faith; resettled her pack on her back and firmly walked towards the wolf expecting anytime for it to spring. But, when she approached without fear, the wolf let her and Ranger pass. Ranger, of course, could not resist looking back over his shoulder, bearing his teeth and growling his own warning...

"Hush boy", he let us pass in peace." Ranger gave a low grunt as if grudgingly agreeing and then took the point staying just a few feet ahead of Elizabeth

She and the dog descended into the cave, and a little way down the path widened and terminated in a perpendicular rock many hundreds of feet wide and equal in height. There was not much light, but by peering directly beneath her, she discovered a pile of sand reaching from the depths below to within ten feet of the top of the rock where she stood.

Holding on to a bush, she swung off from the edge of the rock and dropped onto the sand, sliding rapidly down its steep side into the darkness. Ranger looked down and whimpered his concern. She called to him, reassuringly, and he jumped down onto the sand with her. The trust between woman and dog was back in total.

They landed in a narrow passage running due west through a canyon which gradually grew lighter and lighter until she could see as well as if it had been daylight; but there was no sun. Something in the wall of the cave was glowing. Finally, they came to a section of this passage that was wider for a short distance, and then closed abruptly continuing in a narrow path; just where this section narrowed two huge rattle snakes were coiled, and rearing their heads, hissed at Liz and Ranger as they approached, but neither mistress or dog showed fear, and as soon as they came close to them they withdrew quietly and let them pass.

At the next place, where the passage opened into a wider section, were two angry javalina; a southwest version of a wild boar. But when they approached and Elizabeth spoke to them in gentle

reassuring tones, they stood aside and let
them pass unharmed.

She continued to follow the narrow
passage and the third time it widened and
two mountain lions crouched in the way,
but when she had approached them
without fear and had spoken to them they
also withdrew.

She hesitantly entered the narrow passage. For some time, she followed this trail finally emerging into a fourth section beyond which she could see nothing, but she heard a tremendous clamor. Upon further investigation, she could see that the distant walls of this section were clashing together at regular intervals with tremendous sounds. Ranger, fell behind her, tugging at her back pack, almost urging her to turn back. However, when she approached the rocks they stood apart until she and he had passed.

After this they found themselves in a forest of Saguaro, and following the natural draws, which led westward, soon came into a canyon valley where there were many Indians camped and plenty of game. She saw and recognized many whom she had met in this life, but they seemed oblivious to her presence; as if they were but shadows now of things that had been. A veil was now between them.

Liz and Ranger continued to hike some distance, the pain in Liz's body now intensifying and Ranger staying close to her side as he sensed not only her need but something odd in their surroundings. They had turned onto a small trail that was running into a canyon. Once on this trail, after they had traveled about 25 to 50 yards, they walked into a wall of darkness. Where only moments ago they had been walking in sun shine and mist, now things had dimmed, greatly, and everything was filtered as if she was looking at everything through darkly colored glasses. She noticed that the hackles on Ranger were standing up. Everything in her senses and Ranger's was screaming danger and yet, except for the changes in lighting, nothing looked out of sorts.

Ahead of them, with no way around it, a decaying plank bridge. In the silence of this forbidding place, Liz heard the chants of Noch–De–Klinne and heard a musical voice say "maintain an attitude of respect; you are in a dead zone and are being watched."

Through her training with the Apache, Liz instinctively reached for the medicine bag hanging around her neck.

"That's right"; she felt him say to her. "Make offerings and do the blessings with cornmeal. Open your mind. Let them know that you mean no disrespect and simply want to cross over to the other side. Then sit quietly and turn your attention inward – meditate – see what manifests"

Elizabeth slowly reached into her medicine bag and took out a pinch of cornmeal, dropping it to the ground before her. Ranger stayed close by her side and quietly waited as she dropped to a sitting position on the ground and let her mind open to the hope of what lay beyond this "dead zone"

An oppressive stillness filled the air, very much like the stillness that filled the atmosphere just before the storm that had caused Elizabeth's almost deadly fall. It felt full of vengeful fury and she felt as if her soul were being ripped out of her... And then, just as suddenly, she and Ranger were moved into warm clear sunlight and a feeling of total calm and peace.

Looking around her in absolute disbelief, Liz dropped to her knees and held onto Ranger. "What?" Liz said to Ranger. "What just happened? We did not walk here. How?"

Elizabeth and Ranger were back on the trail they had been exploring so many months ago; leading up to the cave in which she had hoped to find shelter... There was no dilapidated plank bridge, no saguaro forest. It was as though nothing at all had happened.

> However, the scars on Elizabeth's body said much differently.
> As did the pain and extreme fatigue that wracked her entire being.
> As did the moccasins on her feet.
> As did the growth of her Ranger – once a puppy and now a full grown shepherd.

Before the fatigue and pain caused her to pass-out, Liz stretched out her hand and could actually feel the barrier through which she had just crossed. It was cold and hostile and she knew she was never meant to cross it again. Ranger laid himself across his mistress's chest, and fell into a much needed sleep.

FOUND

"Looking behind,
I am filled with gratitude.
Looking forward,
I am filled with vision.
Looking inwards,
I am filled with strength"
~ Quero Apace prayer ~

Sitting on a rock in the area where
Elizabeth's jeep had been found 11
months ago, Jimmy Dale sat silently for
what felt like hours, lost within his mind.
In his dreams, he was constantly hearing
Elizabeth's voice. At night, he often felt

the warm breath of an animal on his face and something pulling on his arm as if to say; follow me. At least once a week for the last 11 months, he had walked the trails of the Superstition Mountains and surrounding wilderness searching for some sign Elizabeth. The only thing the search and rescue teams had ever been able to find of hers was the Jeep; nothing more. The Search and Rescue team and the Pinal Sheriff's department had called off the search for her after two weeks as they felt no one would have been able to survive the excessive heat and monsoons on that mountain longer than that time period. Somehow, in Elizabeth's case, Jimmy just knew they were wrong.

Jon had taken the news with the strength of a true warrior, thought Jimmy Dale. In speaking with Jon, he had been saddened to learn that Elizabeth had requested that, should something happen to her, none of her children or family were to be told; she had nothing left to leave them and did not want to give them bad memories. Jon had her power of attorney and instructions on what to do with her body (still not found) and her belongings. Only Jon...

Driving Jon back to Elizabeth's dilapidated old townhouse in her beloved Jeep Wrangler after the search was called off, Jimmy asked if he could help his new friend in any way.

"No, thank you Jimmy, but I appreciate the offer. For now, I think I will make the rent payments on the place until at least after the Easter holidays and clean up around here a bit before heading back to Wisconsin. I will come back sometime in the late spring or early summer and make the final decisions on what I will keep and what I will sell or give away. I know she wanted all of her belongings that I would not want to keep given to charity, so perhaps in the spring I can call upon you to help me there?" *Then too, he thought to himself, maybe I will just keep the old place and winter here.*

"Oh, and if I leave you a key, could you swing by every so often and keep an eye on the place for me? She was afraid her children might come in and start arguing over stupid things. If they have read the paper, then they know for certain that their mother is gone. She missed them so much... Often, I would sit down stairs and hear her cry for them, but she just could not take the pain or the drama anymore."

"She spoke about it to me quite often Jon. I saw the photos she took and how the light shined in her eyes when she talked of her granddaughter... "

"All I could do was watch her crumble, Jon said. Docs told me the stress made her illness worse..."

Jimmy Dale said, "Oh that part is a fact. The many times I drove her to appointments and she had me stay with her, they said the same thing. Stress was making things worse. "

"Hard to believe these were the same children she talked to me about for years before we ever physically met..."

Jimmy could hear the anger in Jon's voice over the pain Liz had received at the hands of those she loved the most. He could not blame him; he felt the same way. He knew Elizabeth loved them so very much.

"Sure thing", said Jimmy. "Maybe, he added hesitantly," I could even find something for a remembrance of her? Would that be okay? "

"Absolutely", said Jon.

As Jon walked into the house, he turned to look at the cactus garden he and she had planted on the patio. "You know, she loved cactus so much Jimmy. She said they represented "life from death" and the ability to survive; much like she was surviving each battle with cancer. I never thought I would lose her to the desert. We were both so certain that the cancer would take her."

"Hell, I was certain she would out live us all, Jon!" Jimmy Dale responded. "The way she battled back after each surgery... she was one tough cookie our Liz."

They parted as new friends that day and had remained in almost daily contact via text and email ever since. Their connection -- a spirit too soon taken from them who, Jimmy felt, never really knew how important she was to so many.

After the search had been called off, Jimmy could see the light go out in Jon's own eyes. He worried for him, now, as well.

Suddenly, there came the screech of the hawk as it swept low over the Indian's head and glided into the side cave brought Jimmy Dale back to the here and now. The half-breed appeared to almost become one with the bird. He rose to his feet and made his way directly to a deep huge wash.   Literally sliding down in to the wash and then fighting his way back up the rubble on the other side, Jimmy headed directly to the place where the hawk had vanished.

The hawk had come to rest on a rock outcropping just over the cave. It had perched above the drawing of a beautiful Indian maiden with a huge dog at her side. The Indian smiled a knowing smile. He walked faster, as if drawn by some unseen magnet to the base of the painting. There at the base of the painting, in a deeply washed out hole, lay the crumpled unconscious body of Elizabeth and her beloved Ranger; no longer the puppy he knew but a beautiful, full grown dog. Ranger was lying directly across her chest in what Jimmy was certain was an attempt at keeping her warm through the desert night and safe from scavenging coyote or bobcat. Close by, perched on an opposing ledge sat two turkey vultures... waiting.

As he approached, Ranger stirred and came to his feet, ready to defend his mistress. Immediately, he recognized the half-breed and literally leaped in the air with joy and ran up to him.

"Where the hell were you two, boy?" Jimmy shouted as he reached down to warmly pet and embrace the dog. "Look at you, your all grown up!" Let's go check out your mistress now... come on."

Walking over to Elizabeth, she stirred and opened her eyes. She looked at Jimmy Dale and then looked at her beloved Ranger, smiled weakly and whispered; "We're home boy! We're home."

Using his Indian medicines and his knowledge as a medic during the Vietnam War (something he and Jon shared from that terrible war), Jimmy tended the bruised and battered bodies of his friend and her four-legged companion.

However, Jimmy noted that it was evident Elizabeth had already received some type of healing work over the several months she had been missing and she was definitely dehydrated and had lost a great deal of weight.

Dear God, Liz, where have you been? Every one told us to accept that you were dead; but Jon and I... we knew. We KNEW you were alive out here, somewhere. You are a sight for these old eyes. We will get you out of here and back on your feet in no time at all. Damn nation, girl, where the HELL have you been?

Smiling weekly up at Jimmy Dale, she whispered; "you won't believe me when I tell you" and she slipped off into blessed unconsciousness.

Hearing the search helicopter, Jimmy used his mirror to signal for it and then began his chanting prayers of thanks for the spirits for watching over and caring for his dear friend.

When the helicopter arrived, there were only the battered bodies of Elizabeth, and Ranger, and a lone old half breed Apache. There was no wall painting—no Indian Maiden, neither was there a hawk.

When the people, dog, and machinery departed, there was only the silence once again of the Superstitions and the desert.

Jimmy Dale took out his cell phone and made one last call -- to Jon Nickels.

Back in his northern home, Jon looked at the caller ID and noticed it was Jimmy calling. He always held his breath at the initial call; afraid of what he would hear.

He answered the phone, his right hand clenched in fear...

"Jon, this is Jimmy Dale." I have good news my friend. I found her! She is alive but in need of medical attention; She is much thinner, and definitely dehydrated. Her dog is with her. Can you believe it, Jon? She is alive and with the dog! We are taking her by Helicopter now to the Banner hospital in Gilbert."

"Oh thank God! Jimmy I always KNEW she was alive! I knew it. Did you talk with her? Did she tell you where she has been? Did someone have her?" Jon rattled off every question running through his brain without allowing Jimmy Dale a single chance to respond.

Suddenly he remembered that he had to get a flight and pack. "It will take me a few hours but I will be there as soon as I can. I will let you know the flight and all... can you pick me up at the Williams Gate airport?

Absolutely! I will see you soon! And Jon – I always knew she was alive too. Something sacred happened to her out here; a miracle if you will. I am sure we will find out when she is better."

As Jon turned to put his cell phone down and ramp up his computer to check on the earliest flights heading out to Mesa, his right hand unclenched and from it gently dropped a small golden key....

"What the hell is this from?" he said out loud. Shaking his head, he placed the key into his pocket telling himself he would figure out where it belonged later.
Then, Jon called Allegiant Airlines to schedule the next flight out to Mesa; he was going home – this time to stay.

Looking around his house where he had lived for the last 30 years he said "Elizabeth was right! I never belonged here. I belong in the desert!"

EPIPHANIES

And while I stood there, I saw more than I can tell and I understood more than I saw; for I was seeing in a sacred manner the shapes of things in the Spirit, and the shape of all shapes as they must live together like one being. —~Black Elk~

Nature communicates to all people; maybe not all the time, but at least most of the time. It appears, however, that most people are not aware of the communication that is constantly around them. Some who do notice it either don't believe it or they don't understand it. Profound encounters and messages are considered supernatural... or worse, psychotic. Natural signs and omens are considered superstitions and direct experiences are labeled hallucinations.

Chief Dan George was quoted as saying "One thing to remember is to talk to the animals. If you do, they will talk back to you. But, if you don't talk to the animals, they won't talk back to you, then you won't understand, and when you don't understand, you will fear, and when you fear you will destroy the animals, and if you destroy the animals, you destroy yourself"

Are we to believe that Nature itself is not real? Or have we just lost touch with true reality in our pseudo techno world?

Elizabeth, having passed through a Sipapu, had learned to talk with the animals, listen to the wind, praise the sun, the moon, and the stars, and to walk quietly in the unknown surrounded by its beauty and its terrors. She learned that the peace she had sought was always around her; she had just lost touch with it. It took the love of a dog named "No", to help her find it and heal her broken spirit.

One year later, fully healed not only of the injuries suffered in a fall that should have killed her, but miraculously cured from the cancer that had been ravaging her body for several years prior to that fall, Elizabeth walked up a trail into her beloved Superstitions ...

In front of her... a beautiful German shepherd named Ranger; who since their return home had never been called "No" again and who was now spoiled even more then he had been before their journey of renewal and understanding. Beside him, her beautiful 18-year-old granddaughter whose laughter echoed through the canyons.

At her side, her beloved Jon whom she loved with a renewed heart and faith; knowing Hunter had given his blessing and wanted her to live the life she had always been meant to live; on her terms and in her time.

Someday, all of them would pass through a Sipapu again; to spend eternity. Of that she had no doubt... She was living proof they existed and where she, one day, was meant to be.

Finally, even Jon, who had so often professed a non-belief in a life after death, also knew he was meant to be there too. It made the future seem just within reach and warm and inviting

Each day, hope springs eternal.
Each day is wonder-filled
Each day, the Superstitions await.

ABOUT THE BACK COVER
PHOTOGRAPHER JOSHUA KARIE:

Joshua has been a photographer since 2004 and specializes in landscape/ outdoor photography. He holds a certificate in photography. His website is Jkariephoto.com

About the Artist of the Fire Dragon and Owl Man

Originally from Ohio, Alexia Carolann Johnson (Lexi) is a 15-year-old high school sophomore who now resides in Arizona. Passionate about her art, she has been drawing since the age of five; her hope is to one day have a career in the field. Should you wish to reach out to her, you may do so through her grandmother, Sharon Jones, at jsharjean@yahoo.com.

About The Author

By Kim Wright Pritt

Bonnie Pike and Kim Wright Pritt

I have known Bonnie Pike since we were about five years old. At this writing, that makes our friendship approximately 55 years strong. We lost touch a few times over the years, but always seemed to find our way back to each other, as good lasting friendships often do. We have been through a lot together — I was even a bridesmaid at her wedding – so, when she asked me to write the About the Author page for her new book, I thought, "oh, boy, where do I start?"! My strongest and fondest memories of Bonnie in our younger years are from high school. She was always a creative person, with poetry being her main outlet for that creativity. She encouraged me to also try writing poetry, but, alas, poetry was Bonnie's area of expertise, whereas telling stories through my writing was mine. But, I will always remember writing with her and sharing our works. So, I am honored to have been asked to write with her, again – after all these years – by doing this about the author section for her, my dear life-long friend.

Bonnie Pike was born June 8, 1956, in Westfield, New York, to George Tresler and Janice Bemis Gernatt. Two years after being placed into the foster care system at the age two and a half, she was adopted by Edward and Mary Breuilly and grew up in Albion, NY. Which was lucky for me, as that is where we first met in kindergarten not long after she moved in with her new family.

Bonnie met Douglas James Pike in high school when she was only 14 years old and they were married on August 10, 1974. Doug was a career Corpsman in the United States Navy, so they and their three children, Douglas, James, and Mary moved around a great deal as he was stationed in various locations. However, they spent most of their time on the Gulf Coast in Florida. While raising her own children, Bonnie also devoted much of her spare time to working with children in need, such as forming the first successful Cub Scout Pack for mentally and emotionally challenged boys in Pensacola, Florida; pack 645, and being active in the Campfire Kids with the Corry Can-Dos and the Corry Soaring Eagles 4-H group. She also became an AIDS volunteer, working with those living with AIDS, their families, and their significant others to help bring them all some level of dignity as they dealt with the difficult reality of dying.

Bonnie's husband, Doug, became ill and passed away in 1998. They had one grandchild prior to his death, Jessica, and three were born after; James Christopher, Zavier Isaiah, and Shy. Bonnie always likes to say that she is certain that Doug got to hold each of those three grandchildren long before she or even their own mothers and fathers did. Two additional grandchildren joined her family via the marriage of her oldest son to his wife; Michael and Ksondra. She currently resides in Arizona and has realized her dream of living in her own house near her beloved Superstition Mountains and the desert that gives her strength, peace and inspiration.

Losing the love of her life and becoming a widow at such a young age, surviving a history of child abuse, battling multiple severe illnesses with the love and support of a myriad of family and friends, and both the good and bad lessons of life, have given Bonnie many experiences to fuel her creative side and inspire her poetry. She published her first book of poetry in 2002 titled "Survive the Shadow Stalker: A Poetic Journey through Abuse", followed by her second book published in 2011 titled "Shadows of Love, a book of love poems. Her next book of poetry was titled "Dancing with the Spirits of Shadow play", which was published in 2012. Bonnie has also been featured in "The Emerald Coast Review", "The Poet's Voice", "Amelia", "The Back Door Poets Chapbook", "The Panhandler", and "Home Life". She was an active member of the West Florida Literary Federation, serving on their board of directors during her last year in Pensacola, participating in monthly poetry readings at the Backdoor Poets, and producing and directing the Reader's Showcase for over a year.

Now, in her first fictional novel, *A Dog Named "No"* Bonnie draws her inspiration from her beloved Superstition Mountains and her love of Native American cultures and beliefs, particularly that of the Apache. Although fiction woven with history, readers who know her will see much reality weaved into the story. In fact, the protagonist, the dog named No, is based on one of her three German shepherd dogs, Ranger, and the story takes place in the Superstition Mountains. She also pours a great deal of herself into the story…. much like she did in all of her poetry, as well.

After all, Bonnie's life and passion is the basis for all her creative works.

Bonnie presently holds two degrees and was working on a third before cancer and the economy hit hard. She has attended Brockport State University, Troy State University, the University of Phoenix, and Chandler-Gilbert Community College.

Thank you, Bonnie, for giving me the privilege of writing this for your new novel. I wish you luck on this and any future books you decide to pursue. As our friendship has endured through the years, so will your inspirations and stories. Much love to you, always and forever!

485

Made in the USA
Lexington, KY
13 February 2017